HALLOWEEN'S
BLACK MAGICK

The Authentic Grimoire of the Witch of Endor

BASED ON ACTUAL EVENTS

VICTOR BARLOW

Halloween's Black Magick: The Authentic Grimoire of the Witch of Endor

Copyright © 2017 by Victor Barlow
All Rights Reserved.

Trade paperback ISBN: 978-0-9994267-0-8
e-Book ISBN: 978-0-9994267-1-5

Follow Mr. Barlow on Twitter: @Victor_Barlow

This book is published in 2017 by Dark Shadow Press

Visit us Online at: DarkShadowPress.com

For Merek,
you were right.
I should have listened.

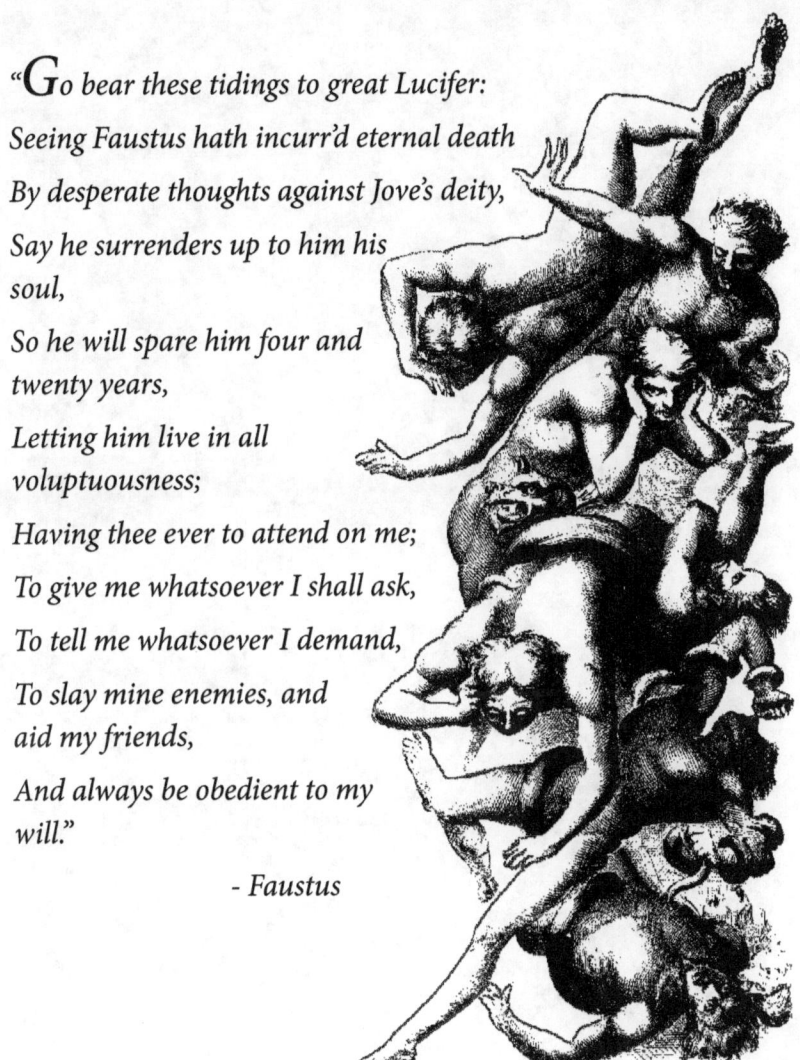

"Go bear these tidings to great Lucifer:

Seeing Faustus hath incurr'd eternal death

By desperate thoughts against Jove's deity,

Say he surrenders up to him his
soul,

So he will spare him four and
twenty years,

Letting him live in all
voluptuousness;

Having thee ever to attend on me;

To give me whatsoever I shall ask,

To tell me whatsoever I demand,

To slay mine enemies, and
aid my friends,

And always be obedient to my
will."

- Faustus

V

Contents

Warning and Disclaimer

The following information described and depicted in this book can be dangerous and could possibly result in serious injury and should not be used or practiced in any way without the guidance of a bona fide kabbalist or occultist.

The author, publisher, and distributors of this book disclaim any liability from loss, injury, or damage, personal or otherwise, resulting from the information and procedures in this book.

This book is for academic study only.

About This Book

"Halloween's Black Magick" is divided into two sections. The first part is the true story of my terrifying encounter with the Witch of Endor that took place in the Fall of 1987. The second part is the Witch's original grimoire that I regrettably took from her nearly thirty years ago.

Endor's Grimoire is the most infamous of all magick books; its existence has eluded historians and researchers for centuries. I have now broken my silence and finally made this compelling book available to the public.

Used with careful discretion, Endor's "Grimoire" contains sigils, incantations, magical formulas, spells (both theurgic and magical), and rituals that will allow you to:

- Summon demons
- Control spirits
- Speak with the dead
- Remove a curse
- Impose nightmares on others
- Cast no shadow
- Levitate
- Countermand Holy Water
- Summon snakes and scorpions
- Ward off enemies
- Teleport
- Change to a Familiar
- Communicate with animals
- Keep your property safe
- And much more

Endor's original grimoire is somewhat disorganized. Unlike modern publications, the subject matter is not neatly organized for ease of use. It is devoid of step-by-step procedures to activate spells and invoke spirits. If you want to reap the benefits found in this book, you'll have to do some work.

The Witch of Endor's Grimoire is also a cryptic book that was originally written in a bastardized mix of Hebrew, Aramaic, and Arabic. To produce the most authentic interpretation of the text, I've managed to secure the help of several well-respected and brilliant linguists to whom I shall forever remain indebted.

For reasons beyond any rational explanation, the publisher and I were unable to photograph the original diagrams and illustrations found in Endor's Grimoire. Each attempt (and there were a lot) at photographing or copying the images failed.

For example, within moments of shooting an illustration, it would always transform into a distorted, misshapen, or burnt image. Was this a strange and consistent photographic anomaly or perhaps something else?

Luckily, however, with the assistance of two talented artists, I have managed to methodically and painstakingly reproduce every image by hand.

Finally, it's my sincere hope that I have presented this grimoire in the manner it so deserves.

MY CONFESSION

Victor Barlow

What I did was wrong.

So much so that it compelled me to write this book. Perhaps it's the guilt, or maybe the fear, that has finally forced me to come clean and tell my story. Regardless of my intention, both conscious and subconscious, this book will ultimately serve as an act of contrition for my selfish actions conducted nearly thirty years ago.

I guess a brief introduction about myself is in order. My name is Victor Barlow, and I have been a teacher of the supernatural and the occult for well over a quarter of a century. I have both formal and extensive training in Kabbalah, Witchcraft, Sufism, Eschatology, and various other esoteric disciplines.

The supernatural has served as both my vocation and avocation. In fact, I've spent a tremendous amount of time and money painstakingly building my library, which contains over one-thousand books and manuscripts. Some are rare and priceless acquisitions.

As a student, I have traveled all over the world seeking knowledge related to any and all aspects of the occult and the dark arts. Much of my youth was spent attending seminary, lectures, and workshops. While my friends were reading Stephen King novels and comic books, I was devouring books like the *Clavicule of Solomon* and the *Book of Honorius*.

As a teacher, I've had the honor and privilege of working in some of the most well-respected schools, imparting my knowledge of the supernatural to eager and open minded students. Hopeful that I would mold the minds of those who would one day join the ranks of my ilk.

My experience with the supernatural is not just limited to the classroom, I've worked as a consultant for both movies and television, including real-life paranormal documentaries.

My encounter with the Witch of Endor goes back to October 1987; I just completed my final series of studies abroad. I was scheduled to head back to the United States later that month and decided to take one last trip.

For as long as I can remember, I've always been fascinated with the Jewish Golem and wanted to visit Prague and tour the old city. For those of you who have never visited Prague, you are missing out. The city is, for lack of a better word, magical. It's a beautiful and ancient place rich with history, legends, and lore that dates back over one thousand years.

Prague is also the most supernatural city in all of Europe. The labyrinth of twisting cobblestone streets along with its magnificent architecture create the perfect storm for black magick.

The myths and legends of Prague are not just limited to the mighty Golem. For example, there's the noble Headless Templar who

In this photo, a view of the old city of Prague.

rides his graceful white horse in the fog-cloaked streets. If you're lucky, you might catch a glimpse of Jáchym Berka, who, every one hundred years, seeks out a virgin girl who will chat with him for one hour. Don't forget the Begging Skeleton, the Mad Barber, and the Ghost of the French Major, to name just a few.

Despite all of the supernatural attractions, I only had time for one tour, and I was determined to learn about the story surrounding the Golem and his mysterious creator.

For those of you who are unfamiliar with the legend of the Golem, it's a fascinating tale. The word Golem has nothing to do with Lord of the Rings. *Golem* is the Hebrew word for "shapeless mass," and it describes a mystical anthropomorphic creature made from mud.

According to Jewish folklore, this towering monster was magically created in the 16th century by the great Kabbalist and Talmudic scholar, Rabbi Judah Loew ben Bezalel. The creature's purpose was to defend the Prague ghetto from anti-semitic attacks and pogroms incited by blood libels (a centuries-old false allegation that Jews slaughtered Christian children, to use their blood for ritual purposes during the Passover holiday).

Fashioned out of mud from the banks of the Vltava River and brought to life through a Kabbalistic ritual, the Golem was an obedient servant who followed every word of its master.

The Golem's powers are nearly God-like. It possessed superhuman strength, boundless endurance, and with skin as hard as a stone, it was virtually indestructible. It was the ultimate superhero.

The legend of the Golem creature is a rich one that is both popular and pervasive. In 1808 the Brothers Grimm wrote a story about a Polish Golem that served as a paradigm for many of the iconic creatures featured in their later folk tales.

After hearing the many stories about the Golem, Mary Shelly was inspired to create her magnum opus, *Frankenstein*.

More recently, many literary historians believe the human-like being Golem was the original inspiration for the introduction of robots and cyborgs into science fiction.

THE GOLEM TOUR

After a bit of research and a couple of recommendations, I decided to go with **Prague Haunted Tours**. They were affordable and reputed to have some of the most knowledgeable tour guides in the city.

My walking tour started in the Old Jewish Quarter of the city and ended at the banks of the Vltava river. I have to admit, the tour was fascinating and our guide was an equally impressive man.

His name was Merek. He was a stout-looking man in his late forties, with an authoritative voice that captured the attention of everyone in our group. His long, dark brown hair was streaked with white. It dangled in front of his bushy eyebrows, which perched on the top edge of his fashionably outdated wire-framed glasses. He wore khaki pants that were too short for his legs and a wrinkled chambray shirt that stretched tightly over his protruding belly.

He pointed his chubby index finger at the twenty-foot statue standing in front of the group. "This is the monument of the Golem's creator, the Jewish mystic, Rabbi Loew of Prague. Also referred to as the Great Maharal," he announced.

Some of the people in our tour rushed towards the massive

Pictured here, the creator of the Golem. A monument in front of Prague City Hall in memory of the Great Jewish mystic, Judah Loew ben Bezalel.

statue, positioning and angling themselves and their cameras for the best shot. Merek continued for several more minutes, and then we moved on.

Highlights of the Golem tour included visiting the Old Synagogue (also called the Altneuschul), where legend states the clay remains of the Golem are stored in its sequestered attic.

Adjacent to the Altneuschul is the Old Jewish Cemetery which is one of the most famous Jewish historical monuments in Prague and considered the largest Jewish cemetery in Europe. Buried here are some of the most venerable rabbis of the past, as well as the great Jewish mystic, Judah Loew ben Bezalel.

I intended to get my money's worth out of the three-hour-long tour. I had many questions for my tour guide and didn't hold back.

Here, the Old Synagogue where it's purported that the Golem's clay remains are stored in a sequestered attic.

Despite my questions, Merek was kind and patient, perhaps even a bit entertained by my zealousness.

Unfortunately, the people in our group didn't feel the same way. I remember how some of them would stare at me with contempt, annoyed that I was holding up the tour, breaking up the continuity of Merek's memorized script.

I just didn't care. I continued with my questions and ignored the frequent stares and obnoxious sighs from the others.

Stupid people, what the hell do they know, I thought to myself. After all, I was a young and brash occultist willing to milk this tour for all it was worth.

In this photo, just a few of the thousands of gravestones which are crammed into the Old Jewish Cemetery in Prague.

A Conversation

After the tour, Merek approached me and asked if he could sit down. I gestured for him to take a seat on the small bench. After a few perfunctory remarks, he asked me about my background. With some tempered humility, I told him about my studies abroad and my passion for supernatural research. I even went so far as to tell him about my book collection back home, not forgetting to casually mention some of my rare collectibles, spanning a broad range of paranormal subjects.

For a few uncomfortable seconds, Merek just stared at me. He smirked and finally looked away, casually observing the remaining members of our tour group as they dispersed into the nooks and crannies of the ancient city.

Merek looked back at me. "So...You like books?"

"Yes, dark books. The kind you seldom see in bookstores," I said.

Merek considered this for a moment and then leaned towards me and whispered, "I know of a place that has such books: ancient ones."

My mouth must have dropped open because I can remember Merek jerking his head away from me when I lunged forward.

"Really? Where? Tell me!" I demanded.

"Calm down!"

Merek explained that it was too dangerous. These books, he explained, belonged to a strange old woman who lives in an abandoned shtetl a few miles outside of the city. The locals won't speak of her, but all of them unanimously agree that she's a witch - but not just any witch. She is the Witch of Endor.

Now, for those of you who need to brush up on your Bible studies, the Witch of Endor, or Endor's Witch, is the most famous ghost story in the Bible.

In fact, the story of the Endor Witch can be found in the book of Samuel, Chapter 28. In this account, King Saul of Israel (who ruled around 1047-1007 BC) was worried about the outcome of his battle with the Philistines on Mount Gilboa. Despite his own prohibition against magick, he sought the assistance of a sorceress to raise the ghost of his predecessor, Samuel. Saul hoped that he could seek advice from Samuel before his battle with his enemy.

According to the Bible, the witch used a talisman to call up the ghost of the recently deceased prophet Samuel. Historians and

The Witch of Endor by Adam Elsheimer.

theologians claim that Samuel's spirit was of little help to Saul. In the end, Saul and his sons were defeated by the Philistines.

But there's more to the story. According to folklore, after the Israelites had been defeated by the Philistines, four of Saul's remaining soldiers went in pursuit of the witch, believing she had cursed their king and his army.

Fearing for her life, the witch fled from the city of Endor and sought refuge in a neighboring town. For twelve days she managed to elude Saul's men.

It wasn't until the thirteenth day that the soldiers encountered a small group of children who told them of the witch's whereabouts. The children spoke of a stranger lurking in town, a mysterious old woman with crimson colored eyes who talked in a foreign tongue.

Acting as judge, jury, and executioner, the soldiers captured the witch and sentenced her to death by lapidation. They stripped her naked, tied her to a tree, and ordered the children to stone the old woman to death.

Legend says the witch suffered for two hours before dying. Her last words were groans of vengeance against the children.

But I digress.

I looked at Merek as if he had two heads. I think I even laughed at him. Frankly, it was so long ago that I can barely remember. It's ironic though, how I've dedicated my life to the world of the fantastical and yet I was doubtful of Merek's claims. The truth is, deep in my bones I'm a skeptic of the supernatural. "Trust but verify" has always been my recessive motto.

I did the math quickly in my head. "Are you telling me a three-thousand-year-old witch is living on the outskirts of the city?"

I was on the verge of cracking a joke but had thought better of it.

Merek shrugged his shoulders. "Believe what you want; it makes no difference to me one way or the other." He became very solemn.

"Are you serious?" I said.

Merek's furry right eyebrow rose high on his forehead. "I'm not making this up. It's the truth. Everyone in Prague knows about the Witch. But they don't speak of her. It's bad luck."

After some delicate and tactful prodding, I got Merek to open up to me. He explained that once a month he delivers food and supplies to the old woman. He drops off the items at her front door and finds his compensation hidden under a rock by the steps.

I asked him if he ever went inside her house, and he immediately snapped back with an emphatic no! Though, he did tell me that once he managed to peek into the side window of her house where he noticed her collection of books.

Despite my initial skepticism, I was intrigued, and after some considerable bickering and one-hundred dollars, I convinced Merek to take me to the crone's house. But he insisted on one caveat. I had to promise him that I would just look at her book collection from outside the window. I was not permitted to enter the house.

I willingly agreed.

THE PLAN

The following night Merek picked me up from my hotel. He was driving a real beater, a Škoda 110 R coupe. The car was a dull orange with random pitted highlights of reddish brown rust. The windshield displayed a large crack that spanned from the driver to passenger side, giving it an eerie, sinister grin. The interior of the vehicle wasn't much better, holes in the cheap vinyl seats, cracked padded dashboard, broken instrument panel, and a rusted out floorboard that allowed a substantial view of the pavement below.

Suddenly it dawned on me that Merek was broke and willing to indulge my obsession for the sake of the almighty dollar. Persuading and seducing someone with money is something I had never done before. It was a strange and unfamiliar concept to me. I felt guilty -- for just a moment.

Heading out of the city was a breeze. We were traveling west, and the traffic was light. Merek didn't say much in the car. I could tell that he was uneasy about the whole thing. I didn't want to push my luck and force a conversation, fearful he would change his mind, so I kept silent during the trip.

I had a lot on my mind during that drive, and I wondered if what I was doing was prudent. After all, I was flying back home to the states the next day. I hated flying, and the mere thought of it made my stomach twist.

God knows I also had a long day ahead of me and I still had a good bit of packing left and logistics to work out before my flight. I just closed my eyes and told myself it would be worth it.

The radio played Bobby Pickett's "*Monster Mash*" through intermittent periods of static. I remember staring out the passenger window, gazing at the ominous orange glow that was cast across the sky, and then it dawned on me that tonight was October 31st: Halloween.

Ironic, I thought to myself.

Now I'd be lying to you if I didn't admit that I was nervous when we drove out that night. For the record, I've never been one for trouble. In high school, for example, while my boisterous classmates were out and about raising hell, I'd be glued to my reading chair enjoying a good book.

I guess you could say that I'm quiet by nature. Perhaps, as some of my exes will testify, I'm even a little boring. I've never been drunk or arrested. I never got into fights. Hell, I never got a speeding ticket.

But I felt comforted in the fact that we had a plan - well, sort of a plan. It was simple enough. First, we would go at night. Darkness would be our ally, or at least, I thought so at the time.

Next, Merek would drive me past the house and park a few blocks away from the place. Then I would approach from the back of the house, take a peek through the woman's window, and get my fill. Finally, I'd get back in the car, and we'd be back in town.

It was as simple as that. No harm, no foul.

15 MINUTES

After twenty minutes of driving, we arrived at a remote village on the outskirts of the city. It was a creepy, desolate place the world had long ago forgotten. Merek pulled over on the side of the road, killed the engine, and turned off the headlights.

He pointed down the road with his finger out the window of the car. "She lives in that small house at the end of the road. The room with the books is on the left side, the side that faces the woods. I'll give you fifteen minutes. If you're not back by then, you'll be on your own."

I listened attentively to every word and glanced nervously at my watch.

"I got it," I said.

"Remember, fifteen minutes. Not a second longer."

He sounded concerned but at the same time detached.

"Okay, okay...I understand."

I yanked at the door handle, stepped out of the car, looked back at Merek and smiled.

"Wish me luck."

Merek just stared at me with mournful eyes. Little did I know, that would be the last time I'd see him.

As I walked through the dark, empty street, crickets hummed monotonously in the brush to my left. I peeked up at the sky one final time and noticed the flaky orange night sky was replaced with smoky gray clouds. A faint damp mist was now in the air.

I looked over my shoulder and could barely see Merek's coupe in the distance. The poor lighting gave his car the appearance of a giant rotten pumpkin covered in the night's mist - bruised, dented, and ready to be crushed and flattened.

The village was spooky, like something out of a zombie flick where everyone is either contaminated with the virus or dead. All of the houses in the village were abandoned and clustered together in tight formation. But the witch's house was a structural pariah, isolated from the others.

In the distance, I could hear howling and barking from wild dogs in the woods. Goosebumps ran over my arms, while a thin sheen of cold sweat covered my forehead and the back of my neck.

My heart raced with anticipation as I surreptitiously approached the small cottage. A dull light glowed through the front window as the rest of the decrepit hovel stood silently in the night. Then, I made my way through a small path that cut through to the side of the house.

Massive, ancient trees hunched precariously over the squalid hut. A sudden gust of wind fluttered the remains of a crow's nest that poked out of the broken chimney. Muted green ivy crawled up the side of the house, clutching and choking it.

Carefully, I walked around the house and zeroed in on the window of the cottage, fearful of being discovered and carefully listening for the sound of approaching footsteps. I stopped in my tracks and quickly looked around. Except for the dead leaves dancing across the weed-choked grass, all was quiet.

A sudden scraping sound rang out. My heart skipped a beat as I looked over my shoulder, discovering the source of the sound; a large branch from a decaying oak tree was clawing against the side of the cottage. I expelled a sigh of relief and continued.

A light sprinkle of rain started to fall as I approached the window on the far side of the house. It was small and slightly ajar. As I leaned forward, I could detect a strange odor coming from the gap in the window. My instincts (you know, the ones we are always taught to trust but always ignore) told me this place was bad, perhaps even dangerous.

I steadied myself and thought, *What harm is there in just looking.*

I slowly lifted my head and peered through the dirt-stained glass. I surveyed the small room. Three thick candles illuminated the place; I saw a small table, human skull, Athame, gold chalice, straight-backed chair, and large makeshift bookshelf standing at the far end of the room.

As Merek had promised, the shelf was loaded with dozens of oversized books. All of them looked ancient, mysterious, and impressive.

But there was something else, something odd that immediately caught my attention. There was a book, sitting on the top of a small wooden desk in the left corner of the room. The book's cover glimmered in the reflection of the candle.

THE WANT

Something suddenly came over me, a powerful desire, an intensely driven *want* that I'd never experienced before. Like a piece of metal being pulled by a magnet, my mind was attracted to this odd-looking book.

While it's difficult to describe, I can only say that I felt like I was in the throes of an uncontrollable trance, perhaps the very same destructive energy that compels a drug addict to shoot smack into his veins or a psychopath to act out. This book had power - a glamour that beckoned me; at that moment I realized I was no longer in control of myself.

Screw it, I thought. *Screw Merek, and screw the witch.*

I wanted a closer look.

Inch by inch I opened the window while my eyes remained fixed on the book.

Stop! Turn around and go back, my rational mind protested. I ignored it and proceeded.

I poked my head through the window and was immediately overwhelmed with the room's cloying smell of death. As my olfactory nerves went into overdrive, I continued, pulling the rest of my body through the small window.

The room was cold, like inside a walk-in freezer. Gooseflesh rippled all over my arms and neck. I remained focused on the book.

Pictured here, artist rendition of Endor's original Grimoire. Notice how the book opens from left to right.

In the back of my head, I knew I was running out of time. I also knew that Merek would not wait for me if I were late. But the book kept calling me. I stepped closer.

My heart raced by the sound of my footfalls. Floorboards creaked and groaned in protest of my weight. Sweat ran down the back of my neck, and I could smell my own fear, the faint yet pungent scent of vinegar emanating from my body.

I continued. Step by step, until I approached the desk.

I paused a moment and looked back at the door of the room. Thankfully it was closed. Without thought, I reached for the wooden chair and wedged it under the doorknob.

If necessary, this would buy me a few precious seconds, I thought to myself.

I took the book from the desktop, assessing its substantial heft and unique construction. The book was made of tattered black leather and brass, it had wooden boards, and its cover adorned with a large silver hexagram, the Star of David. Two leather straps ran across both the top and bottom fore edge of the book, securing its contents.

Reverently, I ran my fingers over the metal Sigil and snapped the metal clasps open. Unlike other books, this one opened from left to right. The pages were made of an ancient paper that emitted the sweet, pungent smell of moldy leaves.

Carefully, I thumbed through the old brittle pages.

Some type of Grimoire, I mused.

Despite my fluency in several languages, I was unable to decipher the book's language. I surmised it was written in an ancient Semitic tongue that was foreign to me. The artwork was also paradoxical, both beautiful and horrible at the same time.

As I mentioned before, I consider myself to be an astute

bibliophile with an extensive collection of occult books. As you might imagine, I'm very familiar with books such as the Munich Manual of Demonic Magic, Heptameron, Grimorium Verum, and the Picatrix. But this book was nothing like the others.

Yes, it had all of the classic signs of a traditional grimoire or book of shadows - anonymous author, cryptic language, bizarre drawings, and puzzling symbols. But *this* book was different, much different.

It had life. A dark existence which radiated a sinister, almost seductively erotic energy of duality. I could feel the pleasure and pain, good and evil, light and dark.

The book was *alive*, and in a matter of a few seconds, I was under its control. I couldn't help the sudden and overwhelming sense of dread.

I glimpsed at my watch, straining my eyes to make out the time.

"Christ, nine-thirty!" I whispered.

I knew that I only had a few remaining minutes before Merek would drive off. I closed the book, took a deep breath, and let it out in a controlled weary sigh. At that very moment, I decided the book was coming with me.

BEWITCHED

One careful step at a time, I made my way back to the window. Then, it happened. The room darkened, and freezing air circulated around me. I turned around and saw an undulating shadow rising out of the filthy floor. Thick darkness continued to fill the room.

I was frozen where I stood, both frightened and amazed as the amorphous shape of black nothingness assumed a human form. It was a malignant energy, a spectre.

At that moment, my body was receiving two contradictory signals from my brain: The first was to run for my life; the second was to stay and observe this once-in-a-lifetime supernatural event. Against my better judgment, the latter prevailed.

I looked up, and there she was, floating three feet above the floor: a tall, frail-looking woman with wildly mussed, wiry black hair. She was wearing a long black threadbare gown that reeked of mildew. The old woman's face was gaunt and had paper-thin, sallow skin.

I'll never forget those red hate-filled eyes that sunk deep into her skull. Those piercing eyes - glassy orbs that indicated a primitive and malevolent intelligence. Her long, sore dappled nose sniffed the air as a dog might do when assessing a stranger, a threat.

She pointed her gnarled index finger at me. I couldn't speak. I was paralyzed with fear.

This isn't real. It's a trick, a Halloween prank, I told myself.

The crone's dry, cracked lips snarled and turned up with a malicious grin, revealing ugly rotting teeth.

"Real as death, you shall see yourself," she replied in a gravelly, wet voice.

But her lips didn't move. She spoke telepathically, and my initial fear instantly turned to sheer panic as my bladder released its warm contents over the front of my jeans. In the dim light, the wet stained denim looked black like tar.

The witch smiled and gave a high, shrill scream that sliced through my brain and chilled my bones. Her breath reeked of rotten meat, and I winced from the overwhelming fetid stench.

Inexorably, her body floated toward me, her filthy dress dragging across the floor. My heart hammered and my body trembled, I tried to scream, but my jaw went slack. I tried to run, but my knees locked. The only physical movement I could manage was to dig my fingers into the surface of the book that was still clasped in my hands.

It was at this point that I fully understood what a deer must feel like seconds before it's struck by an oncoming car. That miserable nauseated feeling of confusion, shock, and hopelessness. And then, the coup de grâce - pain. Unbearable pain.

These were the very same feelings and sensations that ran through my mind and body when the Witch engulfed me. I remember the book falling to the floor as my arms dropped limply to my sides and a great expanse of cold blackness took residence in my brain.

A deep penetrating cold entered my body, convincing me that I was dying. A feeling of deep sadness shot through my tormented mind just seconds before I blacked out.

I fell into a deep phantasmagorical state as I looked through the eyes of some extradimensional being. Unfamiliar names crashed through my mind at the speed of light: *Satanackia, Agalierap, Tarchimache,* and *Fleruty.*

Bizarre images appeared like peripheral flashes of strobing light: a *circle of blood, a massive heap of bones, an inverted cross impaled in the dirt.*

Then, complete blackness, and the sound of distant drums echoing in the absence of light. Perhaps the drums of some ancient army or tribe announcing the call to war.

Boom! Boom! Boom!

There were more flashes of blinding light, and then, a cave appeared. In the damp chamber, ashes floated in the air like dust motes. The place smelled like burnt hair and cooked flesh.

My eyes scanned the area and found the source of the smell. To the right of the cave, there was a large fire pit with a rotisserie spit propped a few feet above it. A human-shaped carcass rotated over the fire, the remains of a female child. Its little body was charred and covered with large heat blisters and dried blood. Unassisted, the spit slowly turned over and over, cooking the witch's long pork.

To the left, a circle of naked children was holding hands, frozen in formation. Their distorted cherubic faces were screaming in horror as thin rivulets of blood cascaded down the corners of their swollen eyes. Poisonous black snakes coiled menacingly around their plump little legs. The ominous sound of war drums continued.

Boom! Boom! Boom!

In the center of the circle stood the red-eyed witch, in full regalia and with a large athame clasped in her left hand. She was laughing and twirling in slow mesmerizing circles as the children's screams set the cadence of her wicked dance. With each horrible twist of her body, I caught the unmistakable smell of rancid meat mixed with damp earth.

She points the tip of her bloodstained knife at a child to her left. The youngster released his grip from the others and floated gracefully to the filthy crone. A boy, perhaps five years old, with golden blonde hair and bright blue eyes. His mouth, agape in frozen horror while his body drifted closer to the evil hag. She continues to laugh and twirl in ecstasy.

The child reaches the witch, his body slowly dips backward, suspending him horizontally in mid-air. Directly below his body was an oversized magick bowl, its rim and exterior drenched in blood.

The witch abruptly stops, closes her eyes, and begins to chant in a low croaky voice. Her words were unintelligible.

As she chants, she slowly raises the knife, now clasped in both of her hands. The head of the child moves slightly back and forth in a futile effort to resist. His eyes widen with pure terror as the drums continue their monotonous beat.

Boom! Boom! Boom!

With both arms stretched above her head, the knife hung menacingly over the child's milky white torso. His plum-sized heart beating frantically against the thin wall of his chest.

The depraved hag slowly opens her eyes and grins, a long thick strand of drool drops from the corner of her mouth, and suddenly...

A Black Rose

I woke up, on the floor of the room, curled up in a tight fetal position. My chest felt heavy and my temples throbbed from the agonizing screams of the children still reverberating in my brain.

I felt a searing pain in my left hand and realized I was clenching the stem of a rose, a black rose, which was both beautiful and ugly. Its razor sharp thorns were deeply embedded in my palm, prompting blood to trickle down my fingers. Instinctively, I threw the flower across the floor and wiped my hand on my shirt.

My stomach immediately lurched, a surge of dark green liquid erupted from my mouth and nostrils, spilling all over the floor. My hand trembled as I wiped the bottom of my sleeve across my chin and mouth. I looked at my pants; the pee stain had already started to dry. Then, at my watch; it was midnight.

My mind was disoriented, and my body was brutally sore. I felt like I went twelve rounds with a vicious heavyweight boxer. My eyes scanned the room. It was empty. Everything was gone - the table, chair, and bookshelf, all were gone. Most importantly, that horrible evil entity was nowhere to be found - the Witch of Endor had vanished.

Fear, rage, and sorrow slammed into me all at once. My eyes started to well up, but I held the tears back.

Did I just experience some horrible nightmare or did someone slip a drug in the dinner I ate earlier? Maybe I was slowly going insane and had just suffered some type of schizophrenic breakdown?

Whatever the reason, I knew I'd address it later. Right now, I just wanted to get the hell out of this place.

Get your shit together, I told myself.

I wasted no time and forced myself to stand on spaghetti legs. My thighs felt stiff and achy. The air in the room felt thick. Despite the moonlight that peered through the open window, dread and darkness still remained with me. I looked around and noticed the cryptic book with the Sigil lying on the floor to my right.

I grabbed it and climbed out of the window.

When I made my way back to the street, I wasn't surprised to see that Merek was gone. A thick patch of motor oil was the only indication that his car had been there.

The thought of the witch entered my mind, sending a chill that ran up my spine.

I clutched the grimoire tightly against my chest and turned around.

Nothing.

No sign of her. Thank Christ!

Something suddenly moved. I saw a large black cat saunter across the street and crawl underneath the rotting floorboards of a deteriorated porch.

Could it be the witch's familiar doing her bidding? Following me.

I thought about breaking into a run and putting some distance between me and the witch's house. I steadied myself and picked up the pace of my walking.

I looked over my shoulder.

No witch. No cat. Just the bleak darkness of night that hovered menacingly over a deserted village.

Then it began. The distant and distinct sound of war drums pounding in the night.

Boom! Boom! Boom!

Wild dogs started howling in concert with the ominous beat, and I knew it was time to get the hell out of Dodge.

The night grew colder, and rain fell steadily as I made my way back to the city; running as fast as my legs would take me.

THE NEXT MORNING

The next morning I had an hour to kill before heading to the airport. I decided to pay a visit to Merek and tell him about what had happened to me the previous night.

A quick walk around Letná Park took me to the Prague Haunted Tours kiosk, a modest setup that sold tickets and provided information about tour dates and times.

A young and attractive woman was working behind the counter. I asked her if she would give a message to Merek for me. She smiled and looked at me, bewildered.

"Who?" she replied.

"Merek...he works here. He gave a tour on the Golem three days ago."

"I'm sorry sir, but there's nobody named Merek who works here."

"Are you sure? He's a short guy, red hair, kind of fat," I said.

"There's nobody like that who works for us, I'm sorry," she replied and went back to her work.

Confused and somewhat disappointed, I wandered around the old city for a little while. Beautiful, fall-colored leaves floated gracefully from the massive oak trees that stretched out above.

A sudden blast of wind sent an explosion of colors into the crisp autumn air: shades of yellow, orange, black, brown, purple, and red. You could almost taste their vibrant colors.

My walk through the park was mindless, and it led me to a vacant park bench, the same one that I had shared with Merek just a couple of days before.

I took a seat and stared into the distance where people were enjoying the fall weather, carrying on with their normal lives: a young couple sharing an ice cream cone, a group of children enjoying a game of tag, a middle-aged man playing fetch with his dog.

These are the mundane activities of life that we take for granted every day. For most of us, our system of reality is never in question; it's pretty much a straightforward experience. We never have to consider or contemplate the inexplicable, illogical or even supernatural. We have the luxury of taking things at face value.

Until yesterday, I was just like these people in the park, living a sane and, for the most part, normal life. But that was then, and now I was faced with an entirely different reality, one that was devoid of universal truths and laws of nature, and it was at this very moment that I realized I was truly alone.

I contemplated the reality of my recent paranormal experience. Did I imagine the witch and those tormented children? Was Merek real? Was the woman at the kiosk lying to me? Was I losing my mind?

If I were going crazy, how does one explain my visit to the old house, the grimoire (that I still have in my possession), and the horrific events that took place the night before? They were real enough, though, as all five of my senses can attest.

I knew that if I were to avoid a complete mental breakdown, I needed to come to terms with everything that I had experienced. I had to immediately institute a paradigm shift that would forever change my way of thinking about the world.

My adult, rational mind had to regress and embrace a new perspective of reality, a child's perspective where a secret world existed by its own rules and where anything is possible.

Analytical and deductive reasoning had to be replaced with imagination, faith, and hope. Anything less would take me down the road to madness.

All of this was still too much to take in at once. I had to digest little pieces at a time, and now, I desperately needed to take a break from thinking about it.

I looked down at my watch, realized I was running late, and walked back to the hotel.

30 YEARS LATER...

So there you have it. Those were the actual events which occurred nearly thirty years ago. Strange, inexplicable phenomena that would ultimately spin my life off course and into utter chaos.

Endor's Grimoire is imbued with black magick power, malevolent energy that would scare the hell out of any seasoned occultist.

When I finally discovered the Grimoire's terrible curse, I tried to destroy it using any and all means (legal and illegal) at my disposal.

I have burned it (repeatedly), ripped it to shreds, and disassembled it piece by piece, only to have it mysteriously reappear in my home, intact and unscathed.

I have dumped it off in libraries, bookstores, and also left it behind in coffee shops and antique stores. And still, the grimoire comes back to me. For a period of time it was like a game, challenging me to come up with new and creative ways to dispose of the book.

For example, I once threw it out of my car driving 75 miles an hour down Interstate 95, tossed it off the Brooklyn bridge, and even submerged it in a barrel of sulfuric acid.

And the same thing happens each and every time, the damn thing reappears a few days later in my living room, bedroom, or the back seat of my car.

Sometimes, I think I can hear the Grimoire laughing at me, taunting me to come up with a better way of destroying it.

I'm certain most of you are probably wondering why I took Endor's Grimoire that night. After all, why would I take ownership of this powerful and disturbing thing? Why would I bring such a dangerous entity into my life?

Well, like all of the forbidden books in my collection, I wanted to study Endor's Grimoire. Perhaps try and understand her magick, make sense of my terrifying experience. Maybe even learn how to harness the grimoire's power - *her* power.

Now, in hindsight, I realize that was a terrible error of judgment. Little did I know that when I took the Grimoire, I unwittingly struck a deal with the devil.

Like Faust, I was a scholar, a self-absorbed man with an insatiable appetite for knowledge. Always hungry, never satisfied, and always searching for more. Knowledge of the supernatural was my drug of choice, and this time I overdosed.

In my defense, I was young and arrogant - tried and true attributes of immaturity. Perhaps I was even a bit careless and stupid. Again, pitfalls of youth that my adult self is forced to accept, but never forgive.

Now, older and hopefully wiser, I must try to attenuate the foolishness of my younger days. This written confession or *proclamation of errors* is my first step.

The second is to release Endor's Grimoire to the public. Perhaps, disseminating its mystical contents will free me of the witch's terrible curse and finally release me of the books ownership.

Because every year, on All Hallows' Eve, a dreadful black rose appears at my doorstep, telling me it's time to pay my dues to the witch; a fee that strips me of my humanity and covers me in blood, lots of blood.

But, that is another story.

Victor Barlow

September 2017
New York

ENDOR'S GRIMOIRE

Ward Thine Enemy

Circle one cubit wide, sigil of Baldan, seven drops of boiled water, asafetida, milk thistle, myrrh. Proclaim:

"I decree fear and pain to others about,

no harm to me, my body, my soul.

Behold, eyes and hoofs of BALDAN,

I trust at my feet.

He guards by day, by night,

by air, by water, by earth, by blood.

So be it."

Deceive Enemy

Dusk of light, Abramelin oil, firelight. Whisper:

"I deliver a trick by thin, by thick.

Cast into my eyes and glamour will beset,

two rocks to one, and one to four

Words of ASTAROTH,

hear what I deem from moon until dawn."

Speak with Tree

Month of Av, juice of etrog, asafetida, tap thrice rod of almond wood, spit to earth. Whisper:

Spirit of trees,

servant of earth come to me,

look down and speak as I decree.

Sun grows weak,

moon turns cold,

talk with me,

as you are told."

Jumping the Path

One day fast, thrice days immersion, inscribe parchment, bury parchment. Full moon, strike ground to north, south, east, west. Meditate [designated] place:

"As sun set,

he comes to this place.

He takes stone of blood, rests by his head,

goes to sleep at his special place.

I invoke thee BEELZEBUTH and SAASIYAH,

serving under the angel PORIHIEL,

in the great name of SHAASHIEL.

Thou bring me to [designated} place,

in the wings of dark angel ASIMON,

quick with speed,

none of pain.

So be it."

Enchant Another

Black rose dust with ink, inscribe on parchment of virgin white. Dawn, parchment by the path of [name], feet walk past:

"Lord of Shadows,

I call unions of lovers past,

in the name of GLUTAB,

over the stars that shine and moon that glow,

of the children of ADAM and legions of KLESTAD.

Offering charms of love of [Name],

for son and daughter, man and wife.

With speed of fire come ye soon."

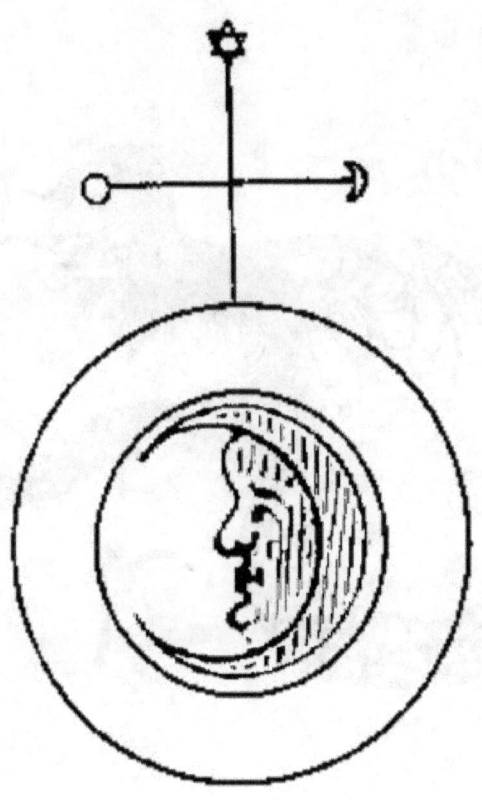

Send forth Aluka (Vampire/Leech)

Star in damp virgin earth, Asafetida, self blood into star. Proclaim:

"Lord of the Darkened Suns,

awaken great ALUKA from earth,

see thy mud as blood,

heed all that I command,

by stealth and by shadow go forth and find.

Lord Estrie, make thy mark in [Name],

and thy soul will forever bind."

Appear Mighty

Hexagram in virgin earth, strike tree thrice with rod of almond wood. Recite:

"Behold giants in days of ATIK YOMIN,

I call upon thee to join thine caste,

SHESHAI, TAMAI heed one, heed all,

engorge me with strength, of size so tall,

I slay mine enemies,

and watch they fall.

Let it be so."

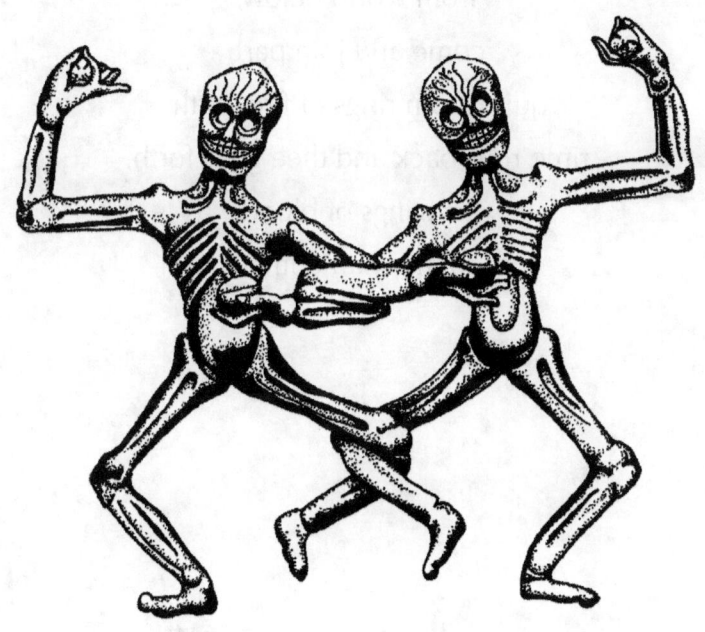

Invoke Asmodeus Spirit Anger

**Deadly roots of Baaras, Asafetida, myrrh, bind in twine.
Drop in fire of full moon. Recite:**

"Awaken great ASMODEUS the great,

from world below,

come and join part,

quick from rings of fire earth,

time rolls back and thee goes forth,

on wings of blood,

to me shall come."

Make Changeling

First night of Adar, doll of wood, straw and turnip, coat with Asafetida, myrrh, hair of mother. Recite:

"My blessings unto thee,

come forth BANEMAN,

come alive this night,

thine mother is gone,

run off from fright,

change now as I command,

I offer you to BAAL,

he who takes flight,

you are mine ceren child,

forever blind to the night."

Change Bat to Demon

Sixth day at twilight, magick bowl, wilderness, firelight.
Chant:

"I summon thee reptile of wings of black,
creature of darkness, flight of night.
I conjure a great change,
I summon the great one IGRAT.
Rise and take your place,
night has fallen,
darkness is your abode,
As I command."

Seeking Counsel with the Dead

Samhain eve, candlewick around the left wrist, three candles, herbs of Dittany of Crete, asafetida, patchouli, knock thrice with rock. Chant:

"I call and summon thee to awaken,

open my eyes so I may see,

open my ears so I may hear.

I summon the one [Name].

Rise before me that I may glace,

speak to me as I will understand,

words of truth.

Rise from the dead,

bring forth wisdom of words of black earth."

To Levitate

Fast one day, circle ten cubit wide, candle, counter step seven times, rod of almond wood. Meditate:

"Spirits of the air,

hear me great one,

and grant my prayers,

A wave of my stick,

and rise from hell.

Grant me separation of earth,

lift me off the ground

"I rise as smoke,

as wind with air.

Grant me the power."

Man to Root

Month of Av, enemy's lock of hair crushed in black rose ash, rotted root weed, asafetida, myrrh, boil, candle. Recite:

"I cast a curse on thee,

boil with root,

with blood and hair,

the change comes soon,

prayers not spare,

With heart and mind,

of soul you will bleed,

time has come,

man as weed."

Awaken Behemoth

Seven times counter walk, firelight, spit saltwater to the east, rod of almond wood. Recite:

"I call thee children of the east,

summon the great beast,

from depths he will swim,

awaken within.

Drink waters of life,

I summon the Behemoth of Job,

awaken from depths of which you swim,

do battle with Leviathan,

of time you will win."

Curse Enemy

Candle wax of crimson, sigil of Solomon, enemy trinket, magick bowl. Meditate:

"Lord of shadows, hear my prayers,

may the evil eye gaze upon him,

may the fevers overtake his mind,

[Name] days are now few,

may others take his position.

May he be fatherless and motherless,

a faceless wonderer of roads of dirt.

Let his children be vagabonds,

extend him no mercy,

no favors or pause.

Prosperity and hope has all but gone.

As I command."

Countermand Holy Water

Holy water, ray of moonlight, white ash, myrrh, rosemary, dark salt:

"I call the spirits of the Air, Earth and Sea,
to deny all strength to water as thee.
In light of moon doth grow stale and not shine,
of all that I possess, it will become mine.
I desecrate this drink as dark as brine,
no power it shall hold,
for now and all time."

Summon Snake/Scorpion

**Full moon in month of Cheshvan, two rocks, candle.
Recite to north, south, east, west:**

"Creature of night that crawl and slither,

from corners of earth draw forth and come hither.

My magick is strong and it calls on thee,

AKRAV,

no obstacle shall impede your path to me,

come now to me as I command."

Change Wind Direction
Rod of almond wood. Recite:

"Winds of North, powerful and light,
change a course and blow with great might,
Winds of South, powerful and light,
change a course and blow with great might
Winds of East, powerful and light,
change a course and blow with great might
Winds of West, powerful and light,
change a course and blow with great might.
As I command, let it be so."

Cast No Shadow

**Magic bowl, firelight, rod of almond wood, self-blood.
Recite:**

"I walk in sun before rays of light,

no shadow shall fall,

I am slight.

No shape will follow,

for I have become one of grey."

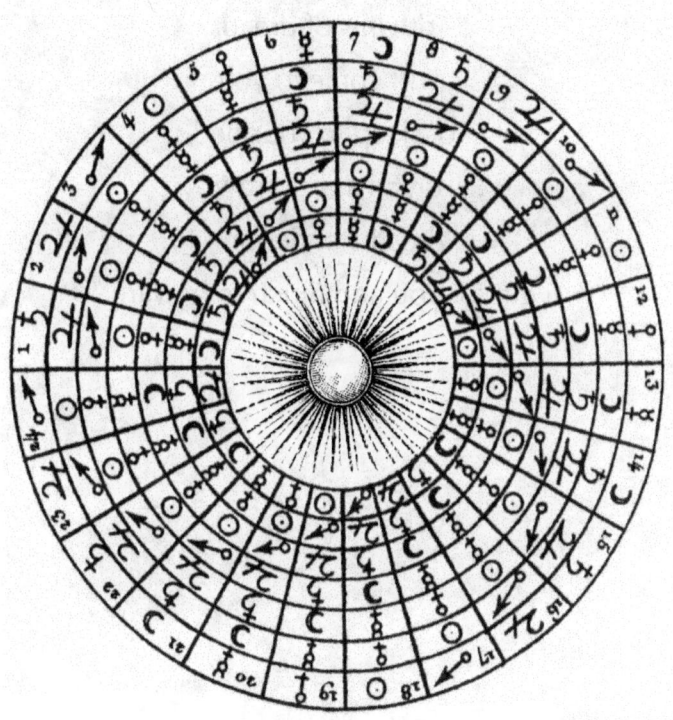

Impose Nightmares on Others

**Charm of flies, agrimony, milk thistle, Abramelin oil.
Recite:**

"Dreams of hate,

dreams of dread,

will come to you,

of sleep in your bed,

dreams of sorrow,

dreams of despair,

a gift for you and much to beware."

Make Another Obey

Full moon in month of Tishrei, letters in virgin black earth, rod of almond wood: Recite:

"I purify in black and state,

Bet is of Alef and two is of one,

Yod, Alef, Bet, Yod, Bet a Vav,

follow thy mind and cast no thought,

Alef a Vav, Bet u Heh,

Bet is of Alef and two is of one.

Obey [Name] and do as I say."

Enter Union of Lucifer

Waxing crescent moon, month of Sivan, magick bowl, herbs of Dittany of Crete, asafetida, myrrh, cloves, hexagram of virgin earth, self blood, rod of almond wood, firelight. Chant:

"By seal of six points of star,

in the name of LUCIFER,

open from earth,

seal of six points of star,

in the name of LUCIFER,

open from earth,

By seal of six points of star,

in the name of LUCIFER,

I open the East,

By seal of six points of star,

in the name of LUCIFER,

I open the West,

By seal of six points of star,

in the name of LUCIFER,

I open the North,

By seal of six points of star,

in the name of LUCIFER,

I open the South."

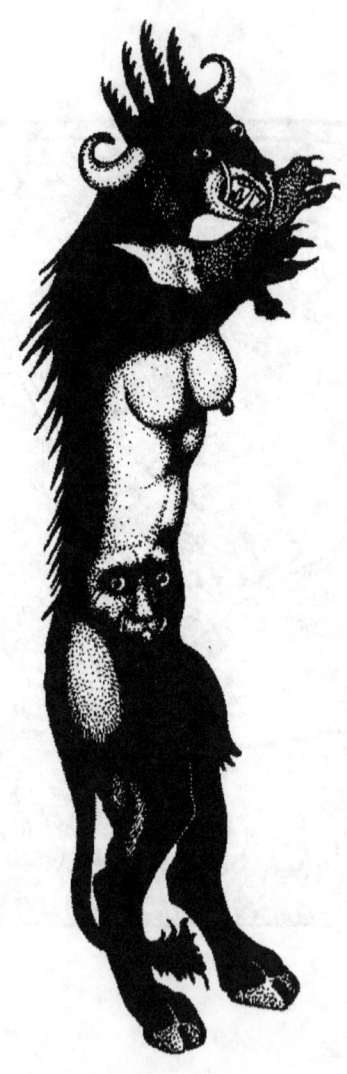

Invoke Huictiigaras

Waxing crescent moon, month of Sivan, hexagram of virgin earth, firelight. Recite:

"By seal of six points of star,

I evoke thee and offer welcome,

HUICTIIGARAS,

Thou art the servant of SYRACH,

teacher and mysteries of sleep,

Let us understand another,

experience of mystery in slumber."

Invoke Clauneck

Waxing crescent moon, month of Sivan, hexagram of virgin earth, firelight. Recite:

"By seal of six points of star,

I evoke thee and offer welcome,

CLAUNECK,

Thou art the servant of SYRACH,

keeper of gold, silver, and treasures,

Let us unite and become aware in sin."

Invoke Musisin

Waxing crescent moon, month of Sivan, hexagram of virgin earth, firelight. Recite:

"By seal of six points of star,

I evoke thee and offer welcome,

MUSISIN,

Thou art the servant of SYRACH,

whisperer of influence and effect,

make words of force travel of sound."

Invoke Frimost

**Waxing crescent moon, month of Sivan, hexagram of
virgin earth, firelight. Recite:**

"By seal of six points of star,

I evoke thee and offer welcome,

FRIMOST,

Thou art the servant of SYRACH,

seducer of females,

give thy power to our work."

Invoke Morail

Waxing crescent moon, month of Sivan, hexagram of virgin earth, firelight. Recite:

"By seal of six points of star,
I evoke thee and offer welcome,
MORAIL,
Thou art the servant of SYRACH,
veiled from eyes that cannot see,
let us share the disguised."

Invoke Guland

Waxing crescent moon, month of Sivan, hexagram of virgin earth, firelight. Recite:

"By seal of six points of star,

I evoke thee and offer welcome,

GULAND,

Thou art the servant of SYRACH,

giver of sickness and malady,

give thy power of illness to our work."

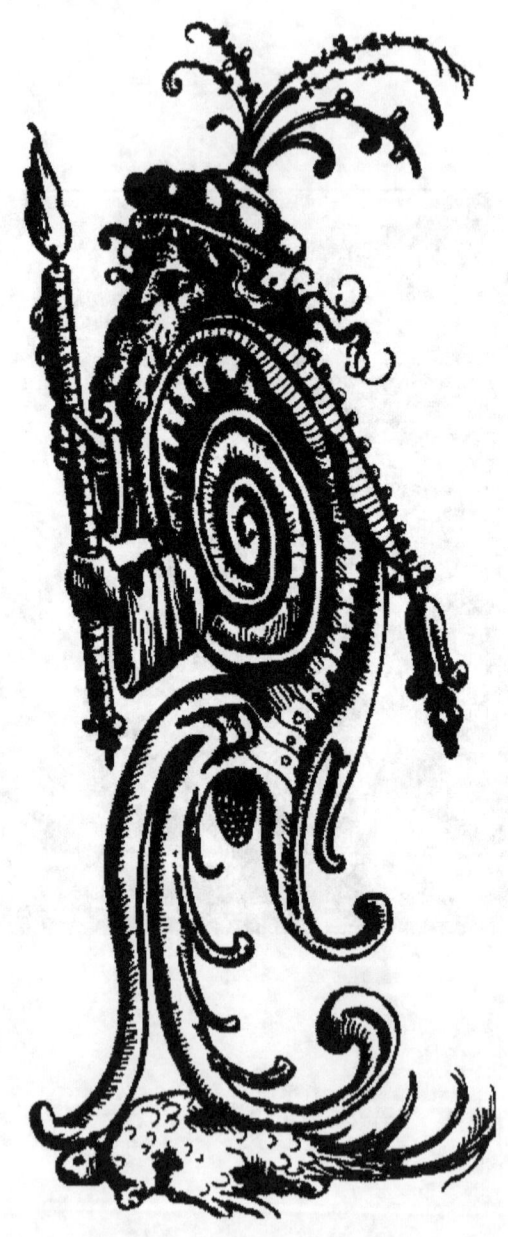

Invoke Humots

Waxing crescent moon, month of Sivan, hexagram of virgin earth, firelight. Recite:

"By seal of six points of star,

I evoke thee and offer welcome,

HUMOTS,

Thou art the servant of SYRACH,

giver of books, make words powerful,

give light of wisdom to my work."

Invoke Hicpacth

Waxing crescent moon, month of Sivan, hexagram of virgin earth, firelight. Recite:

"By seal of six points of star,

I evoke thee and offer welcome,

HICPACTH,

Thou art the servant of SYRACH,

bringer of bodies from far distant lands,

give thy power of travel to my work."

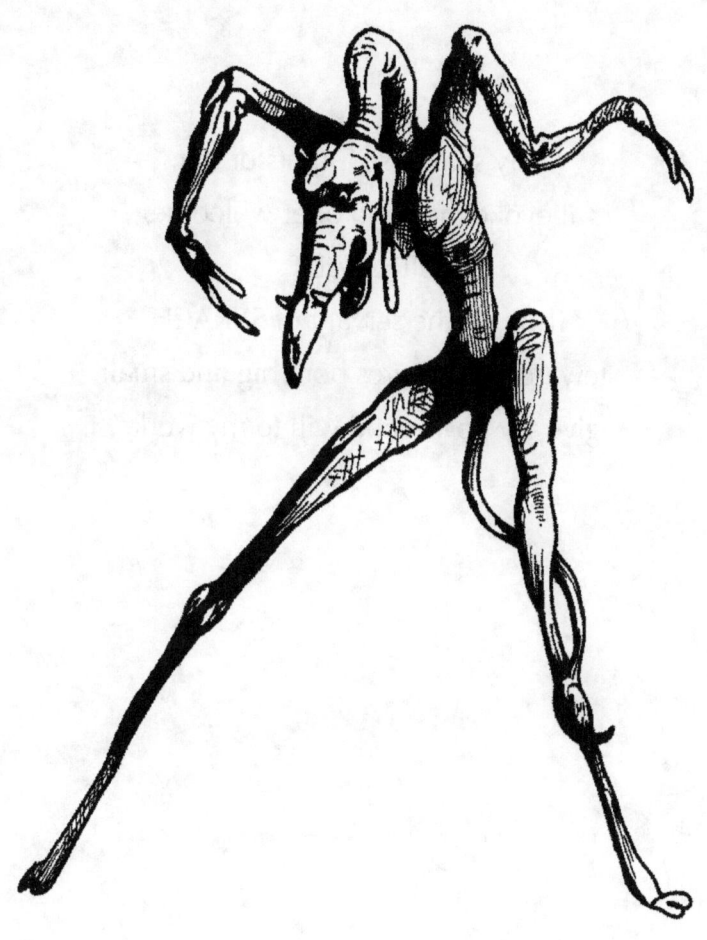

Invoke Sirchade

Waxing crescent moon, month of Sivan, hexagram of virgin earth, firelight. Recite:

"By seal of six points of star,

I evoke thee and offer welcome,

SIRCHADE,

Thou art the servant of SYRACH,

steward of creatures both big and small,

give thy power and will to my work."

Invoke Clistheret

Waxing crescent moon, month of Sivan, hexagram of virgin earth, firelight. Recite:

"By seal of six points of star,
I evoke thee and offer welcome,
CLISTHERET,
Thou art the servant of SYRACH,
ruler of night and day,
give thy power to our work."

Invoke Mersilde

Waxing crescent moon, month of Sivan, hexagram of virgin earth, firelight. Recite:

"By seal of six points of star,
I evoke thee and offer welcome,
MERSILDE,
Thou art the servant of SYRACH,
transporter through starts and moons,
give thy power to our work."

Invoke Khil

Waxing crescent moon, month of Sivan, hexagram of virgin earth, firelight. Recite:

"By seal of six points of star,

I evoke thee and offer welcome,

KHIL,

Thou art the servant of SYRACH,

great shaker of earth,

give thy power to our work."

Invoke Klepoth

Waxing crescent moon, month of Sivan, hexagram of virgin earth, firelight. Recite:

"By seal of six points of star,

I evoke thee and offer welcome,

KLEPOTH,

Thou art the servant of SYRACH,

master of visions,

give thy power to our work."

Invoke Leraje

Waxing crescent moon, month of Sivan, hexagram of virgin earth, firelight. Recite:

"By seal of six points of star,

I evoke thee and offer welcome,

LERAJE,

Thou art servant of SAGATANA,

provoker or battles and contests,

give thy power by seven to our work."

Invoke Frucissiere

Waxing crescent moon, month of Sivan, hexagram of virgin earth, firelight. Recite:

"By seal of six points of star,
I evoke thee and offer welcome,
FRUCISSIERE,
Thou art the servant of SAGATANA,
thee awaken the dead,
give thy power to our work."

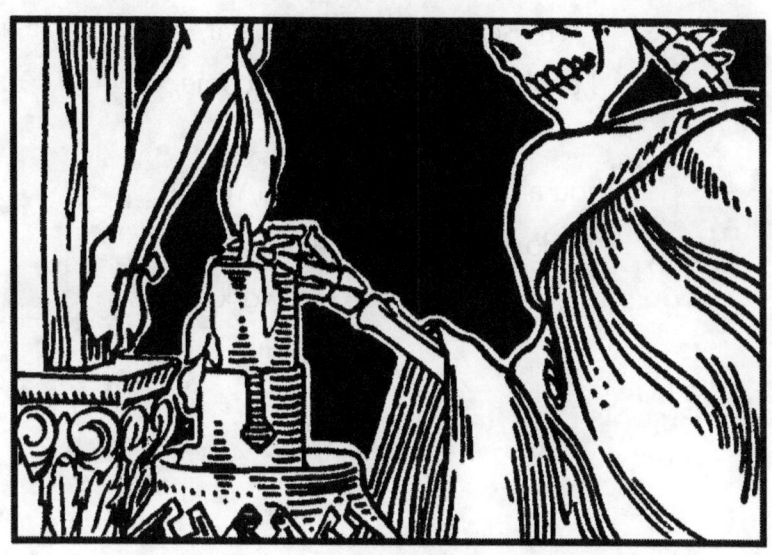

Invoke Surgat

Waxing crescent moon, month of Sivan, hexagram of virgin earth, firelight. Recite:

"By seal of six points of star,
I evoke thee and offer welcome,
SURGAT,
Thou art the servant of SAGATANA,
undo all that is secure and safe,
give thy power to our work."

Invoke Frutimiere

Waxing crescent moon, month of Sivan, hexagram of virgin earth, firelight. Recite:

"By seal of six points of star,

I evoke thee and offer welcome,

FRUTIMIERE,

Thou art the servant of SAGATANA,

provider of feast of sustenance,

give thy power to my work."

Healing Rite

Third hour of night, month of Adar, frankincense, burdock, myrrh. Chant:

"I invoke you,

AVRACHIEL,

The angel of ASUTA and remedy,

In the name of dark one I invoke thee,

do as I ask and restore and cure.

Let it be so."

Bring Sun at Night

Fast one day, hexagram of virgin earth, firelight. Recite:

"Spirits of heat,

I remember you and invoke you,

dark angels that fly above the sun,

fire birthed light,

come now, bring about,

return the rays of sun,

back to the place among black."

Bring Night at Day

Fast one day, hexagram of virgin earth, water. Recite:

"Spirits of darkness,

I remember you and invoke you,

dark angels that fly below stars of pitch,

come now, bring about,

water birthed darkness and covers rays of sun,

make its place with black."

Tribe of Dan Invocation

Waxing crescent moon, month of Tammuz, five pointed star in virgin earth, firelight. Recite:

"By seal of six points of star,
I evoke thee and offer welcome,
TRIBE OF DAN,
fifth son of JACOB
seekers of idolatry,
dance and join my fire."

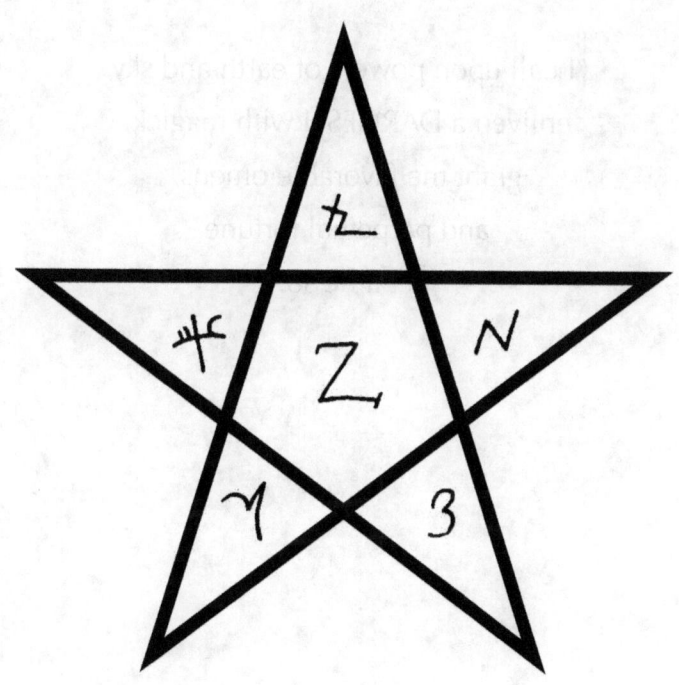

Initiate Dargesh

Month of Cheshvan, hexagram of virgin earth, firelight seven turns, candlelight. Recite:

> "I call upon powers of earth and sky,
>
> enliven a DARGESH with magick,
>
> grant me favorable omens,
>
> and perpetual fortune
>
> Let it be so."

Invoke Domah

Waxing crescent moon, month of Sivan, hexagram of virgin earth, firelight. Recite:

"I call upon angel of the grave,

DOMAH

angel of Gehenna,

punishing angel of the afterlife,

leave thy court,

wave thy scepter of fire,

and visit by my light."

Dybbuk Invocation

Full moon, month of Elul, magick bowl, hexagram of virgin earth, firelight, Abramelin oil. Chant:

"By seal of six points of star,

I evoke thee and offer welcome,

clinging spirit of darkness,

possessor of spirit, body, and mind,

I call upon thee to grant my desire.

Hear my command,

let it be so."

Make Others Forget

Dusk of one hour past, firelight, Magick bowl, Abramelin oil, Asafetida. Recite:

"Spirits of the mind,

be kind to me.

Let thee forget my face,

and neglect my eyes.

Perish all thoughts,

forever a spell is cast about,

I am no more and you will not see.

Let it be so."

Protection Pouch

Quarter moon in month of Elul, black rose dust, deep cloth of black, needle, coarse black thread, cloves, fern, cumin, myrrh, sigil of Solomon: Recite:

"Protection I ask from spirits of darkness,

harness energy and bind in cloth,

I offer a seal of the great and wise.

Instill in pouch of black and scent.

Bless this charm,

grant protection to me,

invoke its protection.

I now decree."

Walk in Stealth

Firelight, magick bowl, black rose dust, Asafetida, hexagram of virgin black earth. Recite:

"I Summon MORAIL,

I provoke no sound and turn no leaf,

my path is silent, presence is meek.

I bring no scent and stir no smell,

for one look at me,

provokes my great spell."

To Destroy Royalty

Fast one day, firelight, magic bowl. Recite:

"By power I invoke this hate spell,

I raise up seekers of discord,

tear down the king

To all rebels I furnish power,

black angels will lead all to error,

for I am the destroyer

Let it be so."

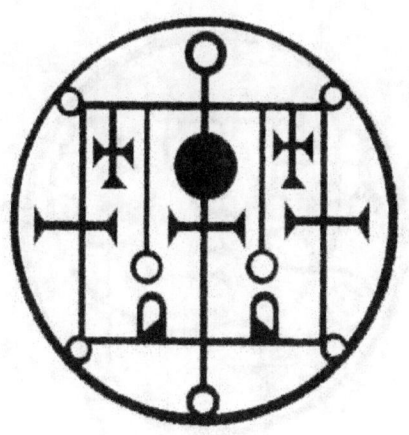

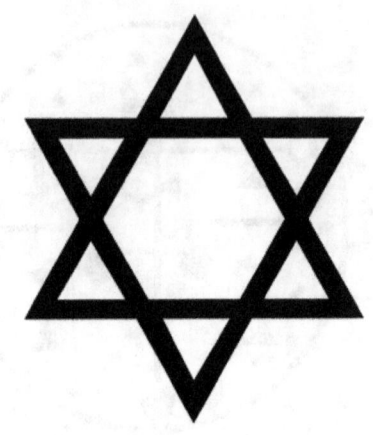

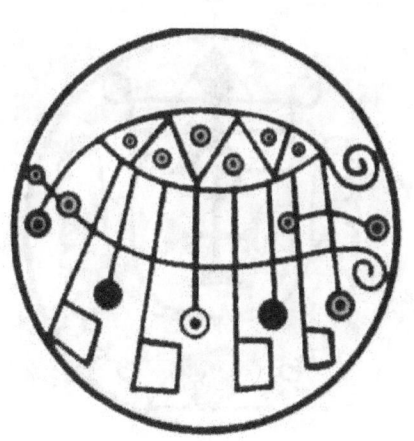

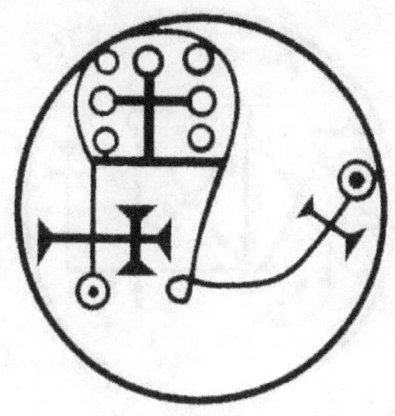

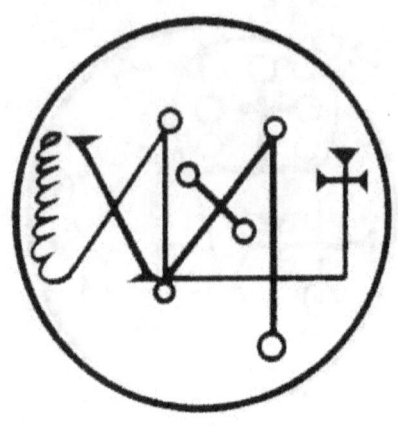

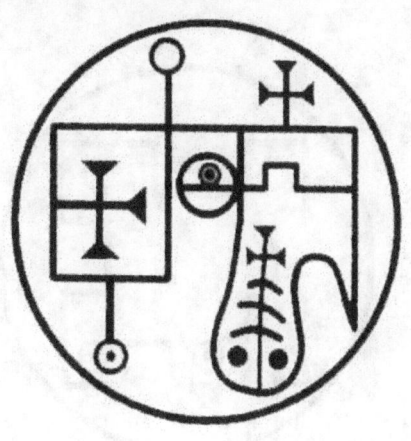

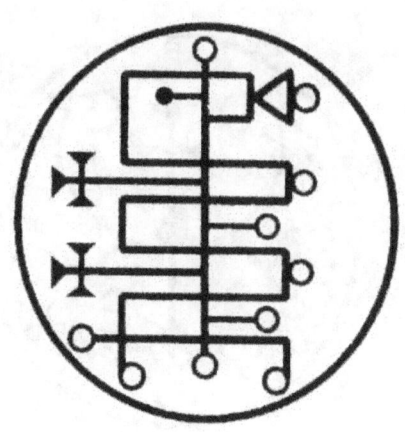

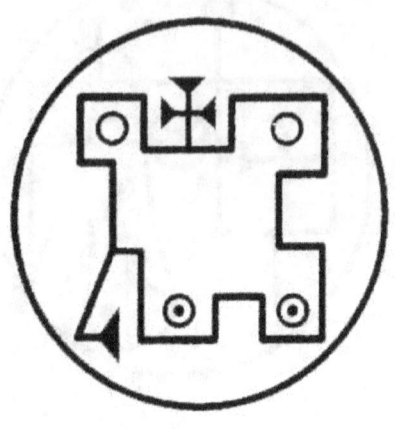

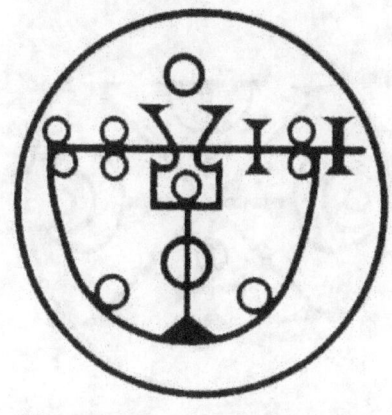

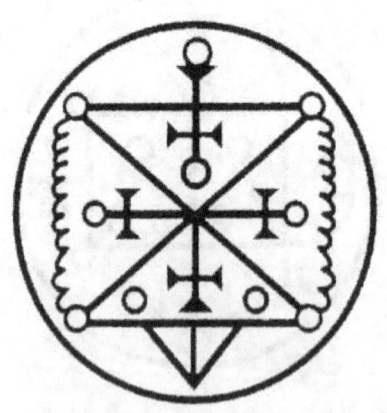

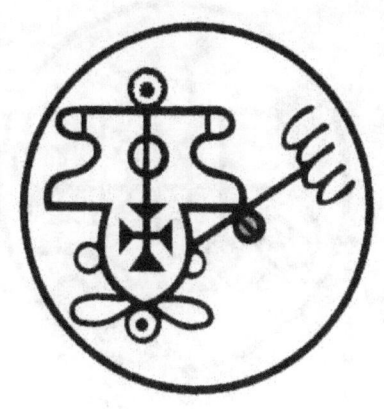

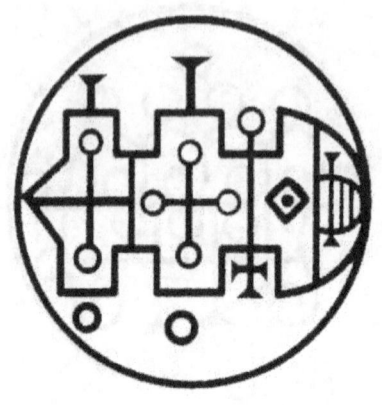

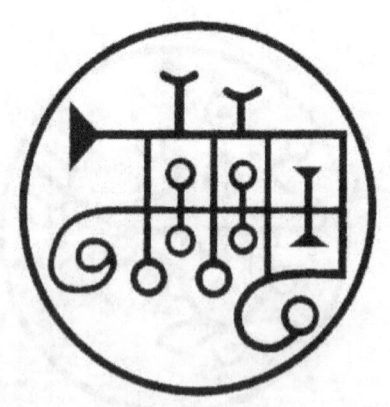

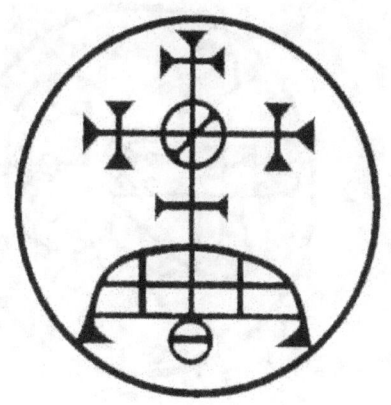

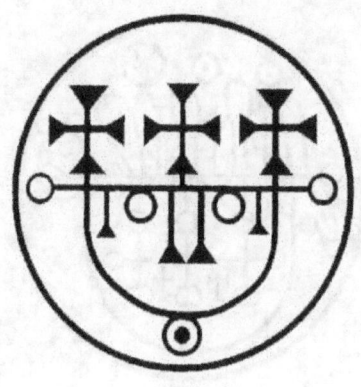

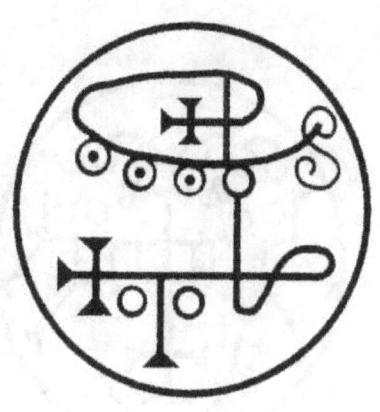

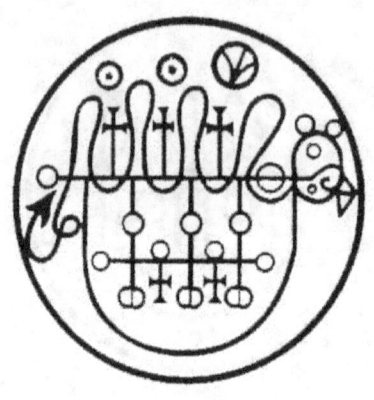

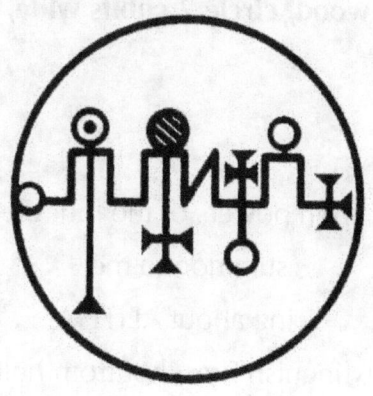

Extinguish Fire

Rod of almond wood, circle 2 cubits wide, black salt, water. Chant:

"I call upon powers of the four elements,

summon to me,

bring about ALITHA,

extinguish fires, hot from hell,

cover the heat,

saturate the light,

bring all to an end.

Do as I command."

Victor Barlow

Invoke Almudhab

Full moon, month of Tammuz, Sunday, hexagram in virgin earth, cardamom, firelight. Recite:

"By seal of six points of star,
I evoke thee and offer welcome,
ALMUDHAB,
gold angel of sun,
provoker of love and friendship,
give power to me,
as I decree.
Let it be so."

150

Invoking Armisael

**Woman's trinket, hexagram in virgin earth, firelight.
Meditate.**

"By seal of six points of star,
I evoke thee and offer welcome,
ARMISAEL,
guard this woman as she bleeds,
the egg of life will hatch you see,
grant desire of my heart,
make all plans succeed."

Summon Hail and Wind

Rod of almond wood, circle two cubits, fist to palm, thrice. Recite:

"I call on thee,

BARADIEL,

angel of hail,

dance across the sky,

come bring rains,

to beat the earth with cold,

blow north to south,

west to east.

Let it be so."

Summon Lightning

Sigil of Solomon in virgin earth, candlelight, rod of almond wood. Recite:

"I call upon thee,

BARAQIEL,

spirit of blue fire,

charge the sky with all thy might,

burn to point,

as I command."

Invoke Demon Queen

Waxing crescent moon, month of Sivan, deadly roots of Baaras, Asafetida, bind in twine, drop in fire. Recite:

"I call on thee,

LILITH,

awaken demon of night,

great queen demon,

open thy door,

hear my prayers and join my fire,

share and speak words of night,

give me study of thy teachings in my heart."

Curse Enemy to Bor

Waxing crescent moon, month of Sivan, hexagram in virgin earth, firelight, enemy's lock of hair, asafetida. Recite:

"By seal of six points of star,

I evoke thee and offer welcome,

AZAZEL,

take my prayers of hate for [Name],

transport and send through starts and moons,

to seventh level of Gehenna,

to Bor of underworld pit.

Let it be so."

Find the Lost

Missing item on parchment, sigil of Solomon, place under head, sleep three nights. Clap hands twice: Recite:

"Hide no more, the mystery of [Name],

for thine eyes can see through cloaks of black,

appear at once as HELTOS commands.

Let it be so."

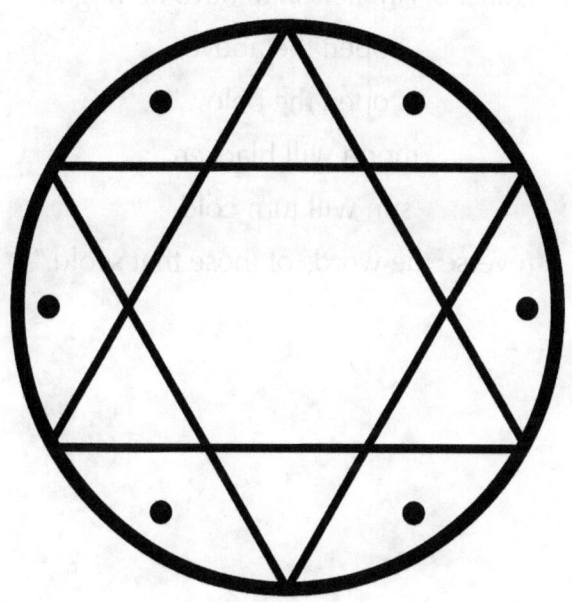

Remove a Curse

Abramelin oil, Asafetida, magick bowl, self-blood. Chant:

"The stars at night, will shine no light.

agents of Amalek shall have no might,

I open the above,

I open the below,

moon will blacken,

sun will turn cold,

I reverse the words of those that scold."

Be Heard in Palaver

Seven almonds in the black earth, inscribe, stomp feet dust rises. Proclaim:

"Give here, oh ye shadows,

I will speak and you will hear,

wind carries my prayers,

rain drops my words,

you shall hear all that is said,

none shall misunderstand.

So be it."

Change to Familiar

Month of Tammuz, firelight, familiar sigil, Abramelin oil, Asafetida. Chant:

"A change in course is what I command,

for what you are now is held in my hand,

Shadows of dust and soil of sin,

turn, change and become my akin.

Let it be so."

Victor Barlow

Bring Forth Rain

Circle half cubit wide, seven drops of water, rod of almond wood. Recite:

"I call on thee,

BAR NIFLI,

son of clouds,

come and bring winds of dark sky,

rain quench thirst of dry earth,

blue fire flash, sky will roar,

birds hide and none will soar,

I shall command,

now it will pour."

Charge the Magick Bowl

**Bowl of clay from fire, inscribe letters of self blood
in bowl, rose dust of black, Asafetida, cloves, sigil of
Solomon in virgin earth, full moon. Chant:**

"In my name you will act.

Seal of SOLOMON will guard this bowl.

Seal of SOLOMON will designate this bowl.

Seal of SOLOMON will charge this bowl.

Bound, sealed and tied by my blood,

this bowl will serve my wishes,

through curse, punishment or desire.

In my name you will act.

Let it be so."

Bring Forth Pestilence

Fast two days, crescent moon, month of Tammuz, hexagram in virgin earth, firelight. Chant:

"Spirit of the deep,

I call on thee,

DEVER,

black against firelight,

demon of plagues,

eclipse the moon and sun,

bring sickness and infestation on all that I see,

As I command,

unleash your wrath.

Let it be so."

Appendix
The Book of Samuel: Chapter 28

In the Hebrew Bible, the Witch of Endor was a sorceress who was ordered by King Saul of Israel to summon the prophet Samuel's spirit. This account can be found in the First Book of Samuel, chapter 28:3–25.

1 And it came to pass in those days, that the Philistines gathered their hosts together for warfare, to fight with Israel. And Achish said unto David: 'Know thou assuredly, that thou shalt go out with me in the host, thou and thy men.'

2 And David said to Achish: 'Therefore thou shalt know what thy servant will do.' And Achish said to David: 'Therefore will I make thee keeper of my head for ever.'

3 Now Samuel was dead, and all Israel had lamented him, and buried him in Ramah, even in his own city. And Saul had put away those that divined by a ghost or a familiar spirit out of the land.

4 And the Philistines gathered themselves together, and came and pitched in Shunem; and Saul gathered all Israel together, and they pitched in Gilboa.

5 And when Saul saw the host of the Philistines, he was afraid, and his heart trembled greatly.

6 And when Saul inquired of the LORD, the LORD answered him not, neither by dreams, nor by Urim, nor by prophets.

7 Then said Saul unto his servants: 'Seek me a woman that divineth by a ghost, that I may go to her, and inquire of her.' And his

servants said to him: 'Behold, there is a woman that divineth by a ghost at En-dor.'

8 And Saul disguised himself, and put on other raiment, and went, he and two men with him, and they came to the woman by night; and he said: 'Divine unto me, I pray thee, by a ghost, and bring me up whomsoever I shall name unto thee.'

Pictured here, Gustave Doré's wonderful illustration of King Saul and the Witch of Endor.

9 And the woman said unto him: 'Behold, thou knowest what Saul hath done, how he hath cut off those that divine by a ghost or a familiar spirit out of the land; wherefore then layest thou a snare for my life, to cause me to die?'

10 And Saul swore to her by the LORD, saying: 'As the LORD liveth, there shall no punishment happen to thee for this thing.'

11 Then said the woman: 'Whom shall I bring up unto thee?' And he said: 'Bring me up Samuel.'

12 And when the woman saw Samuel, she cried with a loud voice; and the woman spoke to Saul, saying: 'Why hast thou deceived me? for thou art Saul.'

13 And the king said unto her: 'Be not afraid; for what seest thou?' And the woman said unto Saul: 'I see a godlike being coming up out of the earth.'

14 And he said unto her: 'What form is he of?' And she said: 'An old man cometh up; and he is covered with a robe.' And Saul perceived that it was Samuel, and he bowed with his face to the ground, and prostrated himself.

15 And Samuel said to Saul: 'Why hast thou disquieted me, to bring me up?' And Saul answered: 'I am sore distressed; for the Philistines make war against me, and God is departed from me, and answereth me no more, neither by prophets, nor by dreams; therefore I have called thee, that thou mayest make known unto me what I shall do.'

16 And Samuel said: 'Wherefore then dost thou ask of me, seeing the LORD is departed from thee, and is become thine adversary?

17 And the LORD hath wrought for Himself; as He spoke by me; and the LORD hath rent the kingdom out of thy hand, and given it to thy neighbour, even to David.

18 Because thou didst not hearken to the voice of the LORD, and didst not execute His fierce wrath upon Amalek, therefore hath the LORD done this thing unto thee this day.

19 Moreover the LORD will deliver Israel also with thee into the hand of the Philistines; and to-morrow shalt thou and thy sons be with me; the LORD will deliver the host of Israel also into the hand of the Philistines.'

Here, Gabriel Ehinger's illustration of Saul speaking to Samuel's spirit at the Witch of Endor, circa 1675.

The Witch of Endor by Nikolai Ge, Circa 1857.

20 Then Saul fell straightway his full length upon the earth, and was sore afraid, because of the words of Samuel; and there was no strength in him; for he had eaten no bread all the day, nor all the night.

21 And the woman came unto Saul, and saw that he was sore affrighted, and said unto him: 'Behold, thy handmaid hath hearkened unto thy voice, and I have put my life in my hand, and have hearkened unto thy words which thou spokest unto me.

22 Now therefore, I pray thee, hearken thou also unto the voice of thy handmaid, and let me set a morsel of bread before thee; and eat, that thou mayest have strength, when thou goest on thy way.'

23 But he refused, and said: 'I will not eat.' But his servants,

together with the woman, urged him; and he hearkened unto their voice. So he arose from the earth, and sat upon the bed.

24 And the woman had a fatted calf in the house; and she made haste, and killed it; and she took flour, and kneaded it, and did bake unleavened bread thereof;

25 and she brought it before Saul, and before his servants; and they did eat. Then they rose up, and went away that night.

Notes

Glossary of Terminology

A

Abramelin oil - also called Oil of Abramelin, is a ceremonial magick oil blended from aromatic plant materials. Its name came about from the medieval grimoire called The Book of Abramelin.

Adar - the twelfth month on the Hebrew calendar, roughly corresponding to the month of March in the Gregorian calendar.

Adept - an individual identified as having attained a specific level of knowledge, skill, or aptitude in doctrines relevant to a particular author or organization.

Akrav - Hebrew word for "scorpion", also a zodiac symbol for the month of Cheshvan.

Alchemy - the medieval version of chemistry, predicated on the supposed transformation of matter. Alchemy is concerned with attempts to convert base metals into gold or to find a universal elixir.

Alef - the first letter of the Hebrew alphabet. In the Gematria, it has the numeric value of one.

Alitha - a supernatural substance or entity capable of extinguishing and fire.

Aluka - Hebrew word for leech.

Amalek - considered both the tribal and spiritual nemesis of Israel.

Amulet - an object or device that is typically worn on one's person, and has magickal power to protect its holder, either to protect them from general danger or to protect them from some specific thing. Some amulets include gems, statues, coins, drawings, pendants, rings, plant parts, animal parts, and even written words in the form of a magickal spell or incantation to repel evil or bad luck.

Animism - animism is the oldest known type of belief system in the world that predates paganism. It is the belief that objects, places, and creatures all possess a unique spiritual essence. Animism perceives all things as animated and alive. Including animals, plants, rocks, rivers, weather systems, human handiwork, and even words.

Arcana - a deck of Tarot cards is divided into two halves or arcanas. The Major Arcana has 22 cards representing dominant events and forces in life. The Minor Arcana (also known as lesser Arcana) has 56 suit cards representing smaller or more mundane life events.

Arka - one of the seven underworld realms mention in the Book of Zohar.

Arzaret - a mythical geographical location in the east, beyond the River Sabatayon, where the ten lost tribes of Israel wait until the arrival of the Messiah.

Ascended Masters - these are spiritually enlightened beings who in past incarnations were ordinary people, but who have undergone a series of spiritual transformations called initiations.

Asimon - a demon or punishing angel mentioned in the Book of Zohar.

Astral Plane - the invisible other world that is unseen from our material world, considered another dimension of reality.

Astral projection - describes a willful out-of-body experience, that assumes the existence of a soul or consciousness called an astral body that separates from the physical body and capable of traveling outside of it throughout the universe.

Astrological aspect - an angle the planets make to each other in the horoscope. Aspects are measured by the angular distance in degrees and minutes of ecliptic longitude between two points, as viewed from Earth. They indicate the timing of transitions and developmental changes in the lives of people and affairs relative to the Earth.

Astrology - the study of the movements and relative positions of celestial bodies interpreted as having an influence on human affairs and the natural world.

Asuta - Hebrew word describing theurgic healing.

Athame - a black-handled, double-edged knife used in witchcraft. The athame appears in certain versions of the Key of Solomon, a grimoire originating in the Middle Ages.

Aura - a human energy field, colored emanation said to enclose a human body or any animal or object.

Augury - the practice from ancient Roman religion of interpreting omens from the observed flight of birds.

Av - the fifth month on the Hebrew calendar which usually occurs in July- August on the Gregorian calendar.

B

Baaras - a mysterious, lethal root found in Israel, used for extracting demons.

Baladan - a demon with the face of a dog mentioned in rabbinic literature.

Balefire - the traditional large open-air fire; a bonfire still used in many pagan celebrations.

Baneman - a doll made of straw that demons substitute for a living child.

Banishing - refers to one or more rituals intended to remove non-physical influences ranging from spirits to negative influences.

Baphomet - a deity, demon and/or symbolic icon which originated in the 14th century as a supposed figure of worship of the Knights Templar.

Behemoth - a beast mention in both the Book of Job and Psalms.

Belomancy - casting of arrows for the purposes of divination.

Besom - a broom usually made of twigs tied around a stick.

Bet- the second letter of the Hebrew alphabet. In the Gematria, it has the numeric value of two.

Bind - to magickally hold; or to restrain something or someone.

Bibliomancy - the use of books in divination. The method of foretelling the future by interpreting a randomly chosen passage from a book, especially the Bible.

Birds - often used as symbols of immortality and the soul.

Black magick - also called "dark magick", has traditionally referred to the use of supernatural powers or magick for evil and selfish purposes. Black magick is considered the malicious, left-hand counterpart of benevolent white magick. Practitioners of black magick are said to be on the "left hand path."

Blood Libel - a centuries-old false allegation that Jews slaughtered Christian children, to use their blood for ritual purposes during the Passover holiday.

Boline - a white-handled ritual knife, one of several magickal tools used in witchcraft.

Book of Shadows - a book of spells, rituals, recipes, and other guides written by a witch or coven of witches.

Bor - the underworld pit, one of the seven levels of Gehenna.

Brontology - divining the future from astrological observation.

C

Cartomancy - a form of fortune-telling using a deck of cards. The most common form of cartomancy is generally tarot card reading.

Tarot cards are almost exclusively used for this purpose. Practitioners of cartomancy are generally known as cartomancers, card readers, or readers.

Ceremonial magick - also referred to as high magick that encompass a wide variety of long, elaborate, and complex rituals of magick. Ceremonial magick is characterized by ceremony and a variety of necessary accessories to aid the practitioner. It draws on such schools of occult thought as Hermetic Qabalah, Enochian magick, Thelema, and the magick of various grimoires.

Chalice - a goblet or footed cup intended to hold a drink, usually wine. In religious practice, a chalice is often used for drinking during a ceremony or may carry a certain symbolic meaning.

Chant - a repeated rhythmic phrase, typically one shouted or sung in unison by a crowd.

Charms - a gemstone, amulet, talisman or other object that has been charged with power for a specific task.

Cheshvan - the eighth month on the Hebrew calendar which usually occurs in October - November in the Gregorian calendar.

Circle - a sacred space in which ritual and magickal workings takes place. A circle may also refer to a loosely organized group of Witches choosing to work together in a less formal manner than a coven.

Clairvoyance - the ability to gain information about an object, person, location or physical event through extrasensory perception.

Cleansing - the process of removing negative energy from an object or place. Cleansing may be accomplished through replacing negative energy with positive energy, such as sweeping with a besom, burning sage sticks, and other means.

Cone of power - a method of raising energy in ritual magick, especially Witchcraft. The term refers to the idea that the raised energy forms a cone with the circle forming its base.

Consecration - the act of cleansing and blessing an object or place by charging it with positive energy.

Coven - refers to a gathering of witches, usually thirteen or fewer, who meet regularly for religious rituals.

Cross of Saint Peter - an inverted Latin cross traditionally used as a Christian symbol, but also used as an anti-Christian symbol.

Curse - any expressed wish that some form of adversity or misfortune will befall or attach to some other entity: one or more persons, a place, or an object. A curse can also refer to a wish or pronouncement made effective by a supernatural or spiritual power. A curse can also be called a hex or a jinx.

D

Da'at or Daas - Hebrew word for Knowledge. In the Kabbalah, Da'at is the mystical state where all ten sephirot in the Tree of Life are united as one.

Dargesh - a good luck charm, often in the form of a bed or a bench.

Demonology - the study of demons or beliefs about demons, especially the methodologies used to summon and control them.

Demon Bowl - see Magick Bowl.

Deosil - clockwise movement of actions in a ritual.

Dever - the demon of plagues.

Divination - the practice of seeking knowledge of the future or the unknown by supernatural means.

Domah - angel of the grave, thought to be a punishing angel.

Drawing Down the Moon - a ritual used during the Full Moon where Witches invoke the power of a Moon Goddess to increase their power.

Dybbuk - in Jewish folklore, a malevolent wandering spirit that enters and possesses the body of a living person.

E

Earth Magick - a form of magick in which the powers of the Earth are sought and used to conduct ritual and mystical workings.

East - symbolizes spiritual and spatial antiquity. Primeval forces are thought to emerge from the east.

Eclipse - eclipses (both solar and lunar) are considered bad omens.

Egg - symbolizes life and immortality.

Elements - considered the four building blocks of the universe. Earth, air, fire, and water, plus spirit. Each is associated with a direction and a color (among other things): Earth (north, green), Air (east, yellow), Fire (south, red), and Water (west, blue), plus Spirit(center, white).

Elul - the sixth month on the Hebrew calendar which usually occurs in August - September on the Gregorian calendar.

Esbat - a coven meeting of Witches on the Full Moon or the New Moon usually to perform rituals. Esbat rituals may also be performed by solitary Witches.

Eschatology - the branch of theology that is concerned with death, judgment, the end of days and the final destiny of the soul.

Esoteric Christianity - an ensemble of spiritual currents which regard Christianity as a mystery religion, and profess the existence and possession of certain esoteric doctrines or practices.

Esoteric cosmology - is cosmology that is part of an esoteric or occult system of thought. Esoteric cosmology maps out the universe with planes of existence and consciousness according to specific world views usually from a doctrine.

Estrie - a Vampire.

Evil Eye - a curse or reification of ill will on another. Also known as the "eye of evil."

Evocation - the act of calling upon or summoning a spirit, demon, god or other supernatural agent, in the Western mystery tradition.

Exorcism - the religious or spiritual practice of evicting demons or other spiritual entities from a person, or an area, they are believed to have possessed. Depending on the beliefs of the exorcist, this may be done by causing the entity to swear an oath, performing an elaborate ritual, or simply by commanding it to depart in the name of a higher power. The practice is ancient and part of the belief system of many cultures and religions.

F

Faerie - one of many nature spirits that inhabit a realm or dimension next to our own.

Fallen Angel - an angel who was cast out of heaven for revolting against God.

Familiars - believed to be supernatural entities that would assist witches in their practice of magick. They would appear in numerous guises, often as an animal, but also at times as a human or humanoid figure.

Fasting - a traditional method of spiritual purification.

Fevers - a form of a demonic attack.

Fire - one of the three elements of creation.

Fish - a symbol of fertility.

Fortune-telling - the practice of predicting information about a person's life.

Fumigation - a form of exorcism using incense to expel a spirit.

G

Gehenna - a spiritual realm of punishment and suffering in the afterlife, also known as Hell.

Gematria - a Kabbalistic system of interpreting the Hebrew scriptures by computing the numerical value of words, names or phrases, based on those of their constituent letters. A good example of Hebrew gematria is the word Chai ("Alive"), which is composed of two letters that add up to 18. This has made 18 a lucky number among the Jewish people.

Geomancy - a method of divination that interprets markings on the ground or the patterns formed by handfuls of soil, rocks, or sand. The most prevalent form of divinatory geomancy involves interpreting a series of 16 figures formed by a randomized process that involves recursion followed by analyzing them, often augmented with astrological interpretations.

Gimel - the third letter of the Hebrew alphabet. In the Gematria, it has the numeric value of three.

Goetia - a practice that includes the conjuration of demons, specifically the ones summoned by the Biblical figure, King Solomon.

Gold - a symbol of eternity.

Golem - the Hebrew word for "shapeless mass", a mystical anthropomorphic creature made from mud. According to Jewish folklore, the creature was created in the 16th century by the great Kabbalist and Talmudic scholar, Rabbi Judah Loew ben Bezalel, to defend the Prague ghetto from anti-semitic attacks and pogroms incited by blood libels.

Gray Magick - magick that is not performed for specifically beneficial reasons, but is also not focused towards completely hostile practices. It is seen as falling in a continuum between white and black magick. It is also called neutral magick.

Grimoire - a textbook or workbook of magick, typically including instructions on how to create magickal objects like talismans and amulets, how to perform magickal spells, charms and divination, and how to summon or invoke supernatural entities such as angels, spirits, and demons. Some grimoires are believed to be imbued with magickal powers.

H

Hail - symbolic of divine punishment.

Hair - a symbol of power and control.

Halloween - or Hallowe'en (a contraction of All Hallows' Evening), also known as Allhalloween, All Hallows' Eve, or All Saints' Eve, is a celebration observed on 31 October, the eve of the Western Christian feast of All Hallows' Day and Reformation Day. It is widely believed that many Halloween traditions originated from Celtic harvest festivals that may have pagan roots, particularly the Gaelic festival Samhain, and that this festival was Christianized as Halloween.

Hate Spell - a specific type of curse that creates hostility between two individuals or groups.

Hexagram - a star-shaped figure formed by two intersecting equilateral triangles. In Judaism, it's commonly referred to as a Magen David or Star of David.

Hex - a curse or any expressed wish that some form of adversity or misfortune will befall or attach to some other entity: one or more persons, a place, or an object.

Histakelut - a form of mental visualization used in Magick.

Homunculus - Latin word for "little man", a representation of a small human being. Popularized in sixteenth-century alchemy and nineteenth-century fiction, it has historically referred to the creation of a miniature, fully formed human.

I

Igrat - a night demon.

Incantation - a charm or spell created using words. An incantation may take place during a ritual, either a hymn or prayer, and may invoke or praise a deity. In magick, occultism, and witchcraft it is used with the intention of casting a spell on an object or a person.

Incantation Bowl - see Magick Bowl.

Incubus - a male spirit or demon believed to have sexual intercourse with sleeping women.

Invocation - a ritual to call on, invoke, or summon a deity or the supernatural.

Iyar - the second month on the Jewish calendar counting from Nissan.

K

Kabbalah - the ancient Jewish tradition of mystical interpretation of the Bible, first transmitted orally and using esoteric methods. Kabbalah reached the height of its influence in the later Middle Ages and remains significant in Hasidism.

Kislev - the ninth month on the Hebrew calendar which usually occurs in November -December.

L

Law of Contagion - a magickal law that suggests that once two people or objects have been in contact, a magickal link persists between them unless or until a formal exorcism or other act of banishing breaks the non-material bond.

Left-Hand Path and Right-Hand Path - refers to a dichotomy between two opposing approaches to magick. This terminology is used in various groups involved in the occult and ceremonial magick. In some definitions, the Left-Hand Path is equated with malicious black magick and the Right-Hand Path with benevolent white magick.

Lucifer - is a name that, according to dictionaries of the English language, refers to the Devil (Satan) or to the planet Venus when appearing as the morning star.

M

Magick - the use of rituals, symbols, actions, gestures, and language with the aim of utilizing supernatural forces.

Magick Circle - a circle, sphere, or field of space marked out by practitioners of many branches of ritual magick, which they generally believe will contain energy and form a sacred space, or will provide them a form of magickal protection, or both. A magick circle may be marked physically, drawn in salt or chalk, for example, or visualized.

Magickal formula - a word whose meaning illustrates principles and degrees of understanding that are often difficult to relay using other forms of speech or writing. These words often have no intrinsic meaning by themselves. However, when deconstructed, each individual letter may refer to some universal concept found in the system that the formula appears.

Magick - a term used to differentiate the occult from performance magic.

Magick bowl -also known as an incantation bowl, or demon bowl, a special type of amulet or talisman used to trap demons.

Maharal - the Hebrew acronym of "Moreinu Ha-Rav Loew", "Our Teacher, Rabbi Loew".

Maleficium - Latin term meaning "wrongdoing" or "mischief", and describes malevolent, dangerous, or harmful magick, "evildoing," or "malevolent sorcery". In general, the term applies to any magickal act intended to cause harm or death to people or property.

Mekubbal - a traditional Kabbalist in Judaism.

Merkabah - a school of early Jewish mysticism that centers on visions such as those found in the Book of Ezekiel concerning stories of ascents to the heavenly palaces and the Throne of God.

Metaphysical - pertaining to realities which are outside those of science.

Mysticism - a belief that union with or absorption into the Deity or the absolute, or the spiritual apprehension of knowledge inaccessible to the intellect, may be attained through contemplation and self-surrender.

N

Necromancer - a person who practices necromancy.

Necromancy - a practice of magick involving communication with the deceased, either by summoning their spirit as an apparition or raising them bodily – for the purpose of divination, imparting the means to foretell future events or discover hidden knowledge, to bring someone back from the dead, or to use the deceased as a weapon, as the term may sometimes be used in a more general sense to refer to black magick or witchcraft.

Nisan - the first month on the Hebrew calendar that falls in March–April on the Gregorian calendar.

Numerology - the belief in the divine, mystical relationship between a number and one or more coinciding events. It is also the study of the numerical value of the letters in words, names and ideas. It is often associated with the paranormal, alongside astrology and similar divinatory arts.

O

Occultism - the study of occult practices, including magick, alchemy, extra-sensory perception, astrology, spiritualism, religion, and divination. Interpretation of occultism and its concepts can be found in the belief structures of philosophies and religions such as Gnosticism, Hermeticism, Kabbalah, Theosophy, Ancient Egyptian religion, Obeah, modern paganism, Eastern philosophy, Western esotericism, and Christian mysticism.

Omen - a phenomenon that is believed to foretell the future, often signifying the advent of change.

Oracle - a person or agency considered to provide wise and insightful counsel or prophetic predictions or precognition of the future.

P

Paganism - a modern religious movement incorporating beliefs or practices from outside the main world religions, especially nature worship: modern paganism includes a respect for mother earth.

Palmistry - foretelling the future through the study of the palm, also known as palm reading or chirology. The practice is found all over the world, with numerous cultural variations. Those who practice chiromancy are generally called palmists, palm readers, hand readers, hand analysts, or chirologists.

Pentacle - an amulet used in magickal evocation, generally made of parchment, paper or metal on which the symbol of a spirit or energy being evoked is drawn. It is often worn around the neck, or placed within the triangle of evocation. Protective symbols may also be included, a common one being the six-point form of the Seal of Solomon, called a pentacle of Solomon or pentangle of Solomon.

Pentagram - a five-pointed star often representing the five Elements of Earth, Air, Fire, Water, and Spirit (the upper point). It may also represent a person with arms and legs spread. Pentagrams are used in many pagan rituals for either positive workings such as invoking one negative ones such as banishing. Inverted the pentagram may represent the Horned God, though it also has Satanist associations.

Planetary hours - an ancient system in which one of the seven classical planets is given rulership over each day and various parts of the day. Developed in Hellenistic astrology, it has possible roots in older Babylonian astrology, and it is the origin of the names of the days of the week as used in English and numerous other languages.

Projective Energy - the energy that one sends out either intentionally or unintentionally. In magick, it is energy that is put into an object or thought-form to achieve one's goals. It is also the energy of power objects that repel negative forces by sending out positive energy.

Q

Qabalah - is a Western esoteric tradition involving mysticism and the occult.

R

Reincarnation - the philosophical or religious concept that an aspect of a living being starts a new life in a different physical body or form after each biological death.

Resurrection - the concept of coming back to life after death.

Rhabdomancy - a divination technique which involves the use of any rod, wand, staff, stick, arrow, or the like.

Ritual - a set sequence of activities involving gestures, words, and objects, performed in a sequestered place.

S

Sabbat - one of the eight festivals observed in the Wicca calendar.

Samhain - celebrated on Halloween, October 31. This celebration marks the New Year, a time for remembering the dead and honoring the Crone Goddess. It is also the final festival of the harvest season.

Satan - the Hebrew word meaning "enemy" or "adversary". A figure appearing in the texts of the Abrahamic religions who brings evil and temptation, and is known as the deceiver who leads humanity astray. Some religious groups teach that he originated as an angel, who used to possess great piety and beauty, but fell because of hubris, seducing humanity into the ways of falsehood and sin, and has power in the fallen world.

Satanism - a group of ideological and philosophical beliefs based on the character of Satan.

Scrying - the practice of looking into a suitable medium in the hope of detecting significant messages or visions. The objective might be personal guidance, prophecy, revelation, or inspiration, but down the ages, scrying in various forms also has been a prominent means of divination or fortune-telling.

Sefer Yetzirah - authored by Abraham, the cryptic Hebrew book containing the magickal incantations and procedures for creating and awakening a Golem.

Sex magick - any type of sexual activity used in magickal, ritualistic or otherwise religious and spiritual pursuits. One practice of sex magick is using the energy of sexual arousal or orgasm with visualization of a desired result.

Shevat - the eleventh month on the Hebrew calendar which usually occurs in January-February.

Sigil - a symbol used in magick.

Sivan - the third month on the Jewish calendar, which usually begins during late May or early June.

Spell - a set of words, spoken or unspoken, which are considered by its user to invoke some magickal effect. Spells can be used in calling upon or summoning a spirit, demon, deity or other supernatural agent, or to prevent a person from taking some action or in forcing them to remain on some path of action (known as binding spell).

T

Table of Correspondences - an esoteric table that lists purported magickal, supernatural, occult, medicinal or similar advice in connection with the subjects being indexed.

Talisman - an object believed to contain certain magickal properties thought to draw good luck to the possessor, or offer the possessor protection from possible evil or harm.

Tammuz- the fourth month on the Jewish calendar, which occurs on the Gregorian calendar around June–July.

Tarot - a set of 78 cards with pictures and symbols that are used for divination by connecting the reader to the subconscious mind.

Tarotology - the theoretical basis for the reading of Tarot cards, a subset of cartomancy, which is the practice of using cards to gain insight into the past, present or future by posing a question to the cards.

Tevet - the tenth month on the Hebrew calendar which usually occurs in December–January.

Therianthropy - refers to the spiritual belief that one has the soul of an animal in their human body or believe they are psychologically or spiritually part animal.

Theurgy - the practice of rituals, sometimes seen as magickal in nature, performed with the intention of invoking the action or evoking the presence of one or more gods, especially with the goal of achieving henosis (uniting with the divine) and perfecting oneself.

Tishrei - the seventh month on the Jewish calendar, which usually occurs in September–October on the Gregorian calendar

Trance - any state of awareness or consciousness other than normal waking consciousness. Trance states may occur involuntarily and unbidden.

U

Underworld - realm of the Dead in Egyptology.

V

Visualization - the process of forming mental images.

W

Wand - a thin, hand-held stick or rod made of wood, stone, ivory, or metals like gold or silver. In modern language, wands are ceremonial and/or have associations with magick but there have been other uses.

Western esotericism - a scholarly term for a wide range of loosely related ideas and movements which have developed within Western society. They are largely distinct both from orthodox Judeo-Christian religion and from Enlightenment rationalism.

Wheel of the Year - the Pagan calendar which symbolizes the eternal cycle of time. It usually begins with Samhain.

White Handled Knife - a knife used by a Witch for craft tasks such as carving candles, making tools, chopping herbs, etc. Though it is not as sacred as the athame, it is reserved for craft work.

Wicca - a modern version of witchcraft based on the old earth Religions of Europe. The term comes from an Old English word meaning "to bend" or "to have wisdom."

Widdershins - counterclockwise motion used in magickal workings or ceremonies. It means to go backward and is sometimes used in banishing magick.

Witch - someone who practices the craft of magick; in using their personal energy with a concentration of will, along with the power and forces of nature, to effect change.

Witchcraft - the practice of, and belief in, magickal skills and abilities that are able to be exercised by individuals and certain social groups. Witchcraft is a complex concept that varies culturally and societally; therefore, it is difficult to define with precision.

About Victor Barlow

A leader in the field of occultism, Victor Barlow has been a teacher of comparative mythology and paranormal studies for over twenty-five years. He has formal training in Jewish mysticism and the dark arts, including Kabbalah, Witchcraft, Sufism, Eschatology, and various other esoteric disciplines.

The supernatural and occult has served as both Mr. Barlow's vocation and avocation. In fact, he's an astute bibliophile with a massive occult library of over one-thousand books. Some of which are rare and priceless acquisitions.

As a student, Victor has traveled all over the world seeking knowledge and wisdom related to all aspects of the supernatural and the dark arts. As a teacher, he's worked in some of the most well-respected schools, imparting his knowledge of the supernatural to eager and open minded students.

Victor's experience with occult practices and paranormal magic is not just limited to the classroom; he has worked in both movies and television. Currently, he's working on a real-life documentary about his horrifying encounter with the Witch of Endor.

Mr. Barlow resides in New York City. For more information about Victor including updates about his books and signing events, you can visit him on Twitter **@Victor_Barlow**

Victor Barlow

216